Claudia refused to feel any guilt

She met his furious stare and said, "We had lunch by the river, and then drove back here." She made it sound very casual. "Satisfied?"

"Was Stephen?" Ellis asked with a sneer that sent a wave of color across her face.

"You've got a disgusting mind!"

"I'm a man myself," he said with an unsmiling shrug. "And a woman like you is temptation with a capital *T!* It didn't occur to me that it would be a mistake to let my brother Stephen meet you. He's never trespassed on my territory before."

"Your territory? I hope you're not referring to me! Because if you are, then let me tell you you're sadly mistaken!"

CHARLOTTE LAMB began to write "because it was one job I could do without having to leave the children." Now writing is her profession. She has had more than eighty Harlequin novels published since 1978. "I love to write," she explains, "and it comes very easily to me." She and her family live in a beautiful old home on the Isle of Man, between England and Ireland. Charlotte spends eight hours a day writing—and enjoys every minute of it.

Books by Charlotte Lamb

A VIOLATION
SECRETS

HARLEQUIN PRESENTS
1202—DESPERATION
1236—SEDUCTIVE STRANGER
1290—RUNAWAY WIFE
1345—RITES OF POSSESSION
1370—DARK PURSUIT
1393—SPELLBINDING
1410—DARK MUSIC
1435—THE THREAT OF LOVE

HARLEQUIN ROMANCE
2696—KINGFISHER MORNING
2804—THE HERON QUEST
2950—YOU CAN LOVE A STRANGER

CHARLOTTE LAMB

heart on fire

Harlequin Books

TORONTO • NEW YORK • LONDON
AMSTERDAM • PARIS • SYDNEY • HAMBURG
STOCKHOLM • ATHENS • TOKYO • MILAN
MADRID • WARSAW • BUDAPEST • AUCKLAND

Harlequin Presents first edition June 1992
ISBN 0-373-11467-2

Original hardcover edition published in 1991
by Mills & Boon Limited

HEART ON FIRE

CHAPTER ONE

CLAUDIA yawned over her breakfast, her green eyes shadowed, and her sister gave her a concerned look. 'You know, you look terrible!' she said with her usual bluntness. 'You're doing too much; it has got to stop. You can't help us in the restaurant every night, and work all day at the hotel; going to bed late and getting up early. You're burning the candle at both ends, and nobody can keep that up for ever.'

'I don't intend to keep it up for ever!' said Claudia, one eye on the clock as she ate hurriedly. The two sisters were eating alone as always. Annette's husband, Pierre, never got up before nine o'clock. He was always the last to go to bed and the last to get up again. Claudia had gone to bed first, but that had still been almost midnight, and her alarm had woken her at seven-thirty, giving her fifteen minutes to shower and dress before breakfast. She was as immaculate as ever, in spite of the haste with which she had dressed; her red-gold hair brushed into a smooth, neat chignon at the back of her fine-boned head, her slender body sheathed in a tailored pin-striped suit with a crisp white shirt, a semi-uniform which was worn by all the secretarial staff employed at the hotel so that guests could distinguish them on sight.

'You don't have to help us out in the restaurant at all!' said Annette, and Claudia made an affectionate face at her.

'When I moved into the flat, we agreed I should pay rent or help you in the restaurant. Until I can afford to pay the rent, I am going to put in a few hours in the restaurant, so stop arguing! I am not living off you and Pierre. Anyway, Joe says he's almost certain I'm going to get that TV stocking advert.'

Annette's mouth twisted. 'That agent of yours is always certain you're going to get some job or other, but you never do!'

'I've had several jobs since I left drama school!' Claudia protested, stung by that. She had had rather more luck in the beginning, actually, with a repertory job in a large seaside town for a whole summer season, and a part in a play on television following that.

'Few and far between, and they never lasted long!' Annette said cynically. The two sisters were very different, both in looks and character. Annette was thinner, taller, her hair darker, although it had a reddish tinge in it, and her eyes were brown. She was down to earth, energetic, very efficient and would have run the lives of everyone around her, if they had let her. Claudia sometimes let her, but more often resisted. Annette refused to believe she had grown up, that was the trouble.

'It's a tough business. It sometimes takes years to get known,' Claudia said defensively. 'And at least I've got a training to fall back on. I'm very glad Dad made me take that secretarial course.'

'You weren't at the time!' Annette reminded, laughing. 'You fought like a tiger to get out of doing it.'

Claudia grimaced. 'I was only seventeen! I've got more common sense now.'

'Then I wish you would take a week off, Claudia. We don't want you to be ill.'

Claudia finished her toast, swallowed the last of her coffee, and got to her feet breathlessly. 'I must rush, I'm on duty at nine—see you tonight.'

Annette called impatiently after her. 'Look, I'm not letting you help us tonight. Understand?'

'OK, thanks, you're an angel, even if you're an interfering one,' Claudia said, yawning again. 'Maybe I'll have an early night. I need one!'

She always walked to work from the flat she shared with her sister and brother-in-law, above the restaurant in Mayfair. It normally took her about fifteen minutes from door to door, but if she hurried she could make it in ten, and today she was in a hurry.

It was a chilly January day. Even if she had had the time to dawdle her way across the park she would have run to keep warm. Her winter coat was very smart, but far too thin; it was second-hand, bought at a charity shop for a few pounds. She bought a lot of her clothes there; it was all she could afford.

She was working, temporarily, as a secretary in a large hotel looking out over St James's Park. She would far rather have been working in a theatre, of course, but, she had to admit, she was enjoying her present job rather more than she had some others she had done since she left drama school four years ago.

Her work was varied and interesting: sometimes she spent the day in the hotel's own office, or was on reception duty; sometimes she was sent to do secretarial work for guests who required help. She met a great many different people, she never knew what to expect each morning when she arrived, and she was well paid. She would have been better paid if she had worked a full week, but she needed a number of hours off each week, to attend auditions, see her voice coach and work out at the dance studio.

As she arrived at the staff door at the back of the hotel, breathing heavily and very flushed after running so fast, she ruefully admitted to herself that her sister was right: she did pack too much into one day, and the strain was beginning to tell. She paused, a stitch in her side, grimacing. Heavens, I feel like going back to bed now, she thought. Let's hope it's going to be a fairly easy working day. I don't think I could cope with a heavy workload today.

She went into the shabby, dark little cloakroom in the bowels of the hotel, hung up her coat, took a quick look at herself in a cloudy little mirror, and went up the stairs. The secretarial staff supervisor looked up from her desk as Claudia came into the large, untidy office overlooking the park. 'Oh, Claudia... at least you're here! Half the staff seem to be down with this flu. I've had three phone calls so far this morning, and half a dozen guests have rung down for secretarial help so we're going to be very busy today.'

Claudia groaned. 'Don't say that, Judy!'

Judy Smith laughed. 'Sorry, but I'm afraid it's true.' A small, neat, spry woman in her late thirties, she had been running this office for ten years. She was good with people and the girls who worked for her liked her.

'Well, what do you want me to do?' Claudia asked, and Judy gave her an uncertain look.

'I just got a call from the Westmorland Suite. A highly skilled secretary is needed there at once, and there isn't anybody else free... Do you think you can cope?'

Claudia wasn't offended by Judy's uncertainty; she knew her secretarial skills weren't first-class. She could type quite fast, and accurately, she could handle a computer, and her shorthand was fairly good, but she wasn't as experienced or fast as some of the girls who worked for the hotel.

'I'll do my best,' she promised, and Judy gave her a grateful smile.

'I know you will. Look, you know a conference starts here tomorrow? One of the multinational corporations...Lefèvre-Bernard, the drug people. Their chairman is Ellis Lefèvre. He brought his own secretary with him but she has gone down with this flu, this morning, so he urgently needs some help typing up a speech he has to make. I think he plans to have another secretary flown over here from Switzerland, where the company is based, but it will take time to get her here and he needs someone now. He expects the very best, and he isn't the easiest man in the world, but he is very important and we don't want to offend or annoy him.' Judy gave her a meaning look. 'He knows the management, I gathered.'

'Oh, he's one of those!' Claudia said, her mouth wry.

'He's trouble with a capital T, Claudia, so be careful!' Judy warned, and Claudia nodded, making for the door.

The Westmorland Suite was the best in the hotel. On the penthouse floor, it had a view of St James's park and gave tantalising glimpses of the upper floors of Buckingham Palace. Claudia rang the bell and after a moment the massive mahogany double door was flung open. A pair of cold grey eyes flickered down over her and she instinctively stiffened, her polite smile freezing on her face.

'Mr Lefèvre? My name is Claudia Thorburn. I ...'

'If you're from the Press, I never give interviews without an appointment,' he brusquely told her, beginning to close the door again.

'No, you don't understand,' Claudia hurriedly said. 'I was sent up by the hotel secretarìal office...'

The door opened again. He gave her another of those swift all-over glances, then his black brows swooped upwards. 'You're the hotel secretary?' He sounded sardonically incredulous. 'I hope you're capable of doing the work! I need someone first-rate. There's a great deal to do, and very little time. Are you fully qualified?'

She opened her mouth to reply but behind him a telephone began to shrill and he gave an irritated sigh. 'Oh, come in... I must answer that.' He strode off, a tall, commanding figure in a dark suit she recognised as expensive, probably made here in London, in Savile Row. She followed him, closing the suite door behind her. He wasn't exactly charming, was he? Judy had said he wasn't the easiest man in the world, and Claudia could see what she had meant.

In the elegantly spacious sitting-room of the suite Ellis Lefèvre was talking in French, on the telephone, his voice even faster, more curt. Claudia knew enough French to follow some of the conversation, and saw that Ellis Lefèvre was fluent in the language. Judy had said that his firm was based in Switzerland, she recalled—perhaps he came from a French-speaking part of the country? Claudia remembered vaguely that Switzerland was divided into cantons, some of which spoke French, some German and some Italian, but she had no idea which was which.

He put down the phone and turned to her impatiently, snapping his fingers. 'Miss...?'

'Thorburn,' she supplied.

He nodded with indifference. 'Right. Miss Thorburn, have you got a pad with you?' He looked at the large pad Claudia at once produced. 'Good, take some notes, will you?' He began dictating a string of notes on the phone call he had just made, and Claudia kept up with him somehow, although she felt hot and bothered by the time he stopped. 'Got that?' he asked, loosening his silk tie. 'Good. Now, take a chair—we have a lot of do, but first I want to ask you some personal questions. The work you will be doing is very confidential and I need to be sure I can trust you.'

Claudia lifted angry green eyes to his face. 'I have worked here for months and there have never been any complaints!'

He shrugged. 'I would still like to know more about you.'

He walked over to a leather-topped desk which had been set up in the corner of the room, and was already covered with papers, a typewriter, telephones, a computer terminal. He sat down on the edge of the desk, picked up a folder and began flicking through the documents it held.

Claudia obediently followed him, sat down, crossing her long, slender legs, her pad open on her knee. Ellis Lefèvre observed the movement over the top of the folder, his cold eyes narrowed, but his face was unreadable. He must be a good poker player, she thought, increasingly finding the man disturbing.

'How long have you worked here?' he demanded.

'On and off for the past couple of years.'

'What do you mean . . . on and off?'

She hesitated, never having discussed her background with a client before, then reluctantly said, 'I'm an actress, as well as a secretary. If I can't get an acting

job, then I work here, but I have a diploma in secretarial work, don't worry. I'm properly qualified.'

His mouth twisted. 'An actress?' Again that cold
glance flicked over her, but she still could not guess
what he was thinking. 'Not a very good one, I gather,
or you wouldn't be working here.' Before she could
react to the dry comment, he went on, 'You're not
married?'

Very flushed now, she shook her head, and he asked
tersely, 'Boyfriend?'

'I don't see why you need to know about my private
life!' Claudia said with resentment.

'I need to know the sort of person you are. Now,
answer my questions quickly, I have no time to waste.'

Claudia furiously muttered replies to the rest of his
questions, wondering if he would want to see her birth
certificate and her driving licence, too.

He fell silent at last and sat, swinging his long legs
and staring at her as if trying to see inside her head.

'Do you know anything about drug manufacture?'
he asked and Claudia shook her head almost
triumphantly.

'Not a thing.'

By now she was hoping he would send her back,
demand that Judy find a replacement. Let someone
else cope with the man!

'Very well, I'll take the risk of trusting you,' he
said, though, to her disgust. 'But heaven help you if
I find you've lied, or you let me down.' The icy glitter
of his grey eyes made Claudia shiver, but she had no
time to wonder what he would do to her if he thought
she had lied to him. For the next hour she felt like
someone riding a whirlwind. His usual secretary had
all her sympathy; she must be an amazing woman if
she could keep up with this human tornado. No

wonder she had gone down with flu. It was probably the first real rest she had had since she started working for him. Claudia was beginning to wish she had flu herself.

The telephone rang every few minutes, and he answered it, his voice curt. He didn't encourage his callers to talk for long.

'Yes?' he would bark, frowning. 'Oh, hello. No, I'm very busy at the moment. Yes, perhaps, later this evening. Lunch? No, I'm afraid I have an appointment... No, dinner's out, too, I'm afraid. Look, I'll give you a ring when I'm free. OK.'

Then he would ring off as soon as possible and go on dictating. The speech was well expressed, she had to admire his grasp of language; it was smoothly constructed, too, but largely incomprehensible to her. He talked about the progress made by the corporation over the past year, delivered some scathing criticisms of mistakes made, went over the successes which had been achieved, thanked those responsible for them, then began to give some breathtaking profit figures, sums Claudia found impossible even to imagine, before going on to sketch the future development of the multinational group over the coming year. Her fingers flew over the page too fast for her to grasp what she was hearing, but she realised that it was definitely privileged information.

At last he leaned back, dropping the folder on to the desk to survey her coolly. 'I want a dozen copies. How long will it take you, do you think?'

She looked over the pages and pages of scribbled shorthand. 'Quite a while. It might have been easier if you had dictated it into a tape machine for me to start work on right away.'

'Anyone can listen to a tape,' he said, his mouth indenting. Shorthand takes time to decipher.' Baffled, she stared, and he gave a sardonic smile.

'There are people who would love to know what I'm going to say before I say it, and I want to make sure nobody gets hold of this speech in advance, so I shall want you to finish keying it into the word processor and get the whole speech printed out before you go home tonight. When you've finished you will place both the copies of the speech and the tape you have used into a large envelope, and put that into the hotel safe and make absolutely certain that nobody knows what you are depositing.' He stood up and began to walk towards the door of the suite, then paused and looked back coolly. 'I have to go out for an hour, so I'm going to lock you in the suite until I get back.'

'Lock me in?' gasped Claudia, beginning to think he was crazy.

'Until I get back,' he said pleasantly. 'I have the only keys on me, by the way. Even the housekeepers can't get in, so don't bother to call them and ask to be let out.'

No wonder Judy had been anxious about sending her up here, Claudia thought. Should she ring Judy and ask to be rescued?

He saw her glance at the telephone on the desk and smiled. 'And all calls are recorded, Miss Thorburn, so unless you want me to know exactly what you are saying when you ring someone, don't make any calls.'

'I shall certainly ring the hotel secretarial office and tell them what is happening,' Claudia defiantly told him, but the threat didn't seem to bother him. He just shrugged.

'Certainly, if you feel you must. Oh, and you can tell them that you'll be spending the night up here, too.'

'What?' Claudia broke out, flushing to her hairline, but she was too late. Ellis Lefèvre walked out of the room, down the wide hallway, and was gone, closing the door of the suite behind him with an ominous click. Claudia ran after him, just in time to see the suite door shut; she tried the handle, uselessly. She hammered on the door, calling out, but there was no reply, and after a while she went back to the sitting-room and dialled the secretarial office number with unsteady fingers.

Judy listened sympathetically, clucking, but only said, 'I'm sorry, love, I did know he was planning to keep you shut into the suite while you did the work. It is very confidential, it seems. If anyone knew in advance what he was going to say it could affect the corporation shares, he said. Anyone who found out could make a fortune on the stock exchange before he made the speech. He has to take extra precautions, just until tomorrow.'

'Why didn't you tell me?' Claudia indignantly asked, and Judy sighed.

'Well, I didn't want to scare you in advance. I thought Mr Lefèvre would explain it much better.' She gave a husky little giggle. 'Isn't he something, though? We don't often have such sexy guests——'

'Judy, all calls are being recorded!' Claudia reminded her grimly, and heard Judy give a little gasp.

'Oh, help! So they are, I'd forgotten!' Hurriedly, she rushed on, 'Now, don't worry, you're quite safe——'

'In prison!' Claudia muttered.

'Oh, I am sorry, dear, but it's a very luxurious cell you've got!' Judy unbelievably giggled, then quickly said, 'And you won't starve! We're sending you up a wonderful lunch.'

'How will you get in? He has the keys.'

'He'll be there, he said he would ring when lunch was wanted. Now I must go, love. I'm so busy, you wouldn't believe it!'

Judy rang off and Claudia slowly replaced the phone, grimacing. Well, that had been no help.

She looked around the suite, which was furnished in classical style, with ivory silk damask curtains and upholstery, a flowered ivory carpet, and gilded Louis XIV furniture. The impression the room made was of lofty calm. It was certainly no hardship to work in a place like this, but she still hated the sensation of being a prisoner.

She went back to the desk, gathered up her notes, and began to work on the computer, feeling like the girl in the fairy-story who has been locked up until she has spun straw into gold. A little smile curled her lips. It would be rather nice if someone appeared and offered to do her work for her. A pity fairy-stories never came true.

Every so often as she worked she remembered Ellis Lefèvre's parting shot, though, and her colour kept changing. She was not spending the night up here. It was bad enough being locked into his suite during the day. She wasn't putting up with being kept here all night. She paused, her fingers poised above the keyboard, her eyes blankly fixed on the VDU, seeing nothing of the words printed on it. Judy had carefully skirted that subject, hadn't she? Judy had admitted knowing Ellis Lefèvre planned to lock her in his suite during the day, but she had made absolutely no comment on his final threat. Had she known about that, too? Surely she couldn't have! Claudia put a hand to her hot face, biting her lower lip. The hotel wouldn't allow a guest to keep a member of the staff in his suite all night. Would they?

All sorts of disturbing ideas began besieging her head. Ellis Lefèvre was a very powerful man, it seemed. He knew the people who ran this hotel. He was rich and used to his own way. Was there no limit to what he could demand—and get—here?

Her face burned. Oh, this was ridiculous! He hadn't given any signs of being interested in her personally. She thought back over the questions he had asked, remembering the way he had looked her over with cool assessment. She couldn't recall any sensuality in that stare. She hadn't felt threatened or alarmed, merely irritated.

But why had he insistently asked if she was married or had a boyfriend? Why had he wanted to know so much about her personal life? Why had he asked if she lived alone, or with others?

The phone rang and she started, but her hand automatically went out to lift the receiver. 'Yes?' she said huskily.

'Is Ellis there?' asked a pleasant-sounding male voice.

'No, I'm afraid not,' said Claudia. 'Can I take a message?'

There was a silence, then the man asked, 'Who is that? Pat, that isn't you, is it?'

'I'm a temporary secretary,' explained Claudia. 'Mr Lefèvre's own secretary is off sick.'

'Poor girl. What's wrong with her? Nothing serious, I hope?' The voice was friendly, full of sympathy, and Claudia decided she liked the sound of it.

'No, it's just flu,' she assured him. 'She should be back at work in a few days.'

'That's good.' A smile sounded in the voice. 'And what's your name, temporary secretary?'

'Claudia Thorburn,' she said, smiling too, because his friendliness was infectious.

'Lovely name—do you match it? What colour hair have you got? You sound like a blonde...are you?'

'No,' she said, unable to resist laughing.

'Aren't you going to tell me? You aren't a brunette?'

'No,' she teased.

'Red-head?'

'You're getting warm! My hair's reddish...and blondish...it isn't a colour that's easy to describe.' She laughed again, then remembered suddenly that this conversation, like all others going through this line, would be recorded. Her smile switched off and she said formally, 'If you tell me your name, sir, I'll tell Mr Lefèvre you rang.'

'I'm Tom Farrell,' he said, sounding faintly puzzled by her abrupt change of mood. 'Look, Claudia, how about lunch...?'

'I'm sorry, I can't,' she said flatly. 'I'll give Mr Lefèvre your message.'

She hung up, her eyes on the screen on which she had been working. What would Ellis Lefèvre make of that conversation? She was flushed, knowing she had been flirting with the man. His voice had such charm, she hadn't been able to help herself. Oh, well! What of it? she thought defiantly, it was none of Ellis Lefèvre's business. She made herself go back to work, refusing to think about Ellis Lefèvre any more. When he returned she would demand that he let her go, and she didn't care if she lost her job in consequence.

It must have been half an hour later that she heard the outer door being unlocked. Stiffening, Claudia listened to the sound of footsteps, then Ellis Lefèvre appeared in the sitting-room doorway.

Her smouldering expression seemed to amuse him. His grey eyes glinted and his brows curved in mockery.

'How is the work coming?' he merely asked, however.

'I'm more than a quarter of the way through it,' she coldly said.

'Then you should finish it today.' He took his jacket off and tossed it on to a chair. 'Any phone calls?'

'Yes, one from a Mr Tom Farrell. He didn't leave a message.'

Ellis Lefèvre eyed her thoughtfully, his brows meeting, then leaned over the desk and touched a switch on the telephone. There was a whirring sound, then Claudia heard her own voice, and bit her lip. He hadn't been lying when he had said that every call would be recorded. But then she hadn't thought he had lied. He was very close to her, that lean body casually draped over the desk. Out of the corner of her eye she could see the powerful tanned column of his neck, the hardness of his profile. She saw the cynical twist of his lips, too, as he listened to Tom Farrell flirting with her, and her own soft laughter. Thank heavens she had remembered their conversation was being recorded!

The recording switched off and Ellis Lefèvre swivelled to look at her. 'I don't want you talking to Tom Farrell or seeing Tom Farrell for the next couple of days—is that understood?'

Claudia resented the high-handed command, and could not believe, anyway, that Tom Farrell was not as charming and likeable as he sounded. Frowning, she said, 'No, I don't understand. Doesn't he work for you?'

He looked impatient. 'Oh, yes, he works for the corporation,' he agreed. 'But that's no guarantee that he is trustworthy.'

Claudia was almost speechless. The man was simply incredible! 'Well,' she said logically, 'If you don't trust him, why don't you fire him?'

'Because it's wiser to keep your enemies where you can watch them,' he told her drily.

'You want to keep everyone where you can watch them!' muttered Claudia. 'That sounds awfully like paranoia to me!'

He gave her a narrow-eyed glance. 'You have a dangerous tendency to say just what is in your mind, Miss Thorburn. Let me advise you to control it.' He saw the defiant glitter of her eyes and her mouth opening to answer back, and talked over her. 'Now, get on with your work, will you? I've got some phone calls to make before lunch.'

'Yes, sir,' Claudia said, her green eyes rebellious, and looked back at her screen while he sauntered out of the room. A moment later she heard the distant sound of his voice, now very familiar to her, clipped and rapid, and always with that undertone of sarcasm which made the little hairs on the back of her neck prickle with irritation.

She had never met a man she felt she could actually loathe, but Ellis Lefèvre might well be the first one. It must be all that money that made him think he could snap his fingers and everyone would jump. No doubt some people would love to know the contents of this speech of his; it was clearly loaded with valuable information about the corporation he headed, and anyone knowing about it in advance might be able to make a fortune on the stock exchange. Claudia did not really doubt his judgement over that, but she resented being locked up here in his suite all day, and nothing would make her stay here all night.

He came back into the sitting-room a few minutes later and she looked up at once, belligerence in her face. 'Mr Lefèvre, I am not staying in this suite all night! I won't tell anyone about the speech. You have to take my word for it——'

'Too much depends on total discretion,' he said curtly. 'I'm sorry, I realise it will be inconvenient, but you must stay here until I actually get up on to my feet in the conference hall.'

'You can't make me!' she snapped, flushed and angry.

He smiled coldly, and she felt a strange shiver run down her spine, but before he had answered somebody knocked on the outer door of the suite, and Ellis Lefèvre looked at his watch, then strode out of the room. Claudia heard him open the door, heard a woman's warm, throaty voice, heard the unmistakable sound of a lingering kiss.

'Darling...' the woman said. 'Aren't we going down to lunch after all? I don't mind if we stay up here, of course...' She laughed softly. 'But my father is waiting for us in the restaurant, we must ring down and tell him if we aren't joining him.'

Ellis sounded cool and down to earth. 'We are, Estelle. I took my jacket off because the suite was so overheated, that's all. I must have a word with your father about this central heating. It ought to be turned down a good five degrees. Hang on, while I get my jacket.'

He came back into the sitting-room, his long legs covering the ground at astonishing speed, and Claudia watched sideways as he picked up his jacket, without so much as glancing in her direction, and turned to leave again.

From the door the woman's voice said laughingly, 'You have an amazing eye for detail, darling, don't you? Nothing is too unimportant to escape your attention. Don't they say that Napoleon was like that? He was always ready to solve the tiniest problem, even in the middle of a battle! I suppose it's part of the drive to success, you . . .' Her voice tailed off as she came further into the room and suddenly noticed Claudia.

Her face changed and so did her voice; the husky softness went out of it and a domineering tone entered. 'Who's that?' she demanded. She had been smiling and suddenly she wasn't.

A tall, slender brunette in a smart white wool dress, she had dark eyes which took on the hard glitter of jet as she surveyed Claudia from head to toe, not liking what she saw, judging by her expression. Claudia could return the compliment. She did not like the other woman much, either.

'She's one of your girls!' Ellis Lefèvre drawled indifferently. 'My secretary has gone down with flu and I have a mass of work to get through while I'm here, so I asked your secretariat to send up someone to do the typing.' He sounded far from enthusiastic about Claudia, and the other woman began smiling again.

'Oh, dear, I'm afraid quite a few of our own staff have got this vicious type of flu that is going around, so we're short-staffed and can't always provide our best girls for the moment. I hope she's doing the work adequately, though?'

Stiff with indignation, Claudia pretended to be engrossed in her work and unaware of what they were saying. She had never once set eyes on this girl—who on earth could she be? Ellis Lefèvre had called her Estelle—but the name meant nothing to Claudia. Could she be the daughter of one of the directors? Or a major shareholder in the hotel company? Claudia was sure she was not the manager's daughter, because she had to be in her mid-twenties and the manager himself was not much more than forty.

She kept talking as if she knew all about the hotel, and how it was run, though—did she work somewhere in the building? This was a very large hotel and there were still many departments of it with which Claudia was not yet acquainted. If she hadn't yet run across this Estelle it didn't mean she didn't work here.

Ellis shrugged. 'She had better do a good job!' he said, turning away, his eyes on his watch. Claudia gave him a look which should have gone right through his shoulder-blades, but of which he seemed blithely unconscious.

Somebody rang the suite doorbell and as if he had been expecting it Ellis Lefèvre was already on his way to answer it before Claudia actually heard it.

'Oh, no, who can that be?' groaned the dark girl. 'Darling, don't let anyone start up one of your boring business discussions. My father will be sending out search parties if we aren't downstairs soon!'

Ellis didn't answer; he had disappeared into the hallway of the suite. 'Thanks,' his voice said to someone. There was a murmur in reply, and Ellis said crisply, 'No, thank you, nothing else.' The suite door closed and Ellis walked back into the room, pushing in front of him a table loaded with food.

'What's this?' said the dark girl in surprise. 'Darling, you hadn't forgotten we were lunching together?'

'No, it's for her. I don't want her wasting time going out for lunch so I told them to send something up for her.'

Claudia's teeth met. He talked about her as if she couldn't hear him; was deaf, dumb and blind—a robot, perhaps! Not human, anyway, and with no feelings or rights. The cool arrogance made her want to hit him.

The dark girl lifted a silver cover and pulled a half-bottle of wine out of an ice bucket, her eyebrows lifting. 'For her? Ellis, you must be heaven to work for! Or didn't you explain that the meal was only for your secretary?'

Claudia shot her a fiery look from under lowered lashes. Now she was doing it! She would love to tell them both what she thought of them, but she didn't, of course. She kept on working, her face carefully blank.

Estelle began walking to the door. 'Come on, darling! I'm starving, looking at all this lovely food!'

Ellis Lefèvre looked at Claudia and said, 'Eat your meal or it will be ruined.' Before she could answer he was on his way out of the suite. She heard their voices, then the outer door closed and she was alone again. It seemed very quiet and she felt oddly depressed, she couldn't think why. Maybe because she had been in a rage a moment ago and had had to bottle it up, so that now she felt flat and bored. She felt lonely too; she felt as if she were on a desert island.

She certainly wasn't hungry, but she got up to investigate the food on the table, lifting the silver cover, as Estelle had done, and finding that Ellis had ordered her a large sole, with prawns in a creamy sauce on the side of the plate. Or had he simply told the kitchen to send up something for her, and had they chosen the dish? She put the cover back, to keep the foot hot, and went to the bathroom to wash, then came back and sat down to eat. It was boring eating alone, but the luxury of the beautifully laundered damask napkin and tablecloth, the white roses in a small, thin glass vase, the white wine and the elegantly presented food, certainly helped to fight her strange depression.

She loved the avocado and fresh orange, thinly sliced in a fan with a garnish of feathery dill; the sole, served with a trio of *nouvelle cuisine* vegetables, crisply cooked and sculpted into shapes, with which she drank her one glass of wine. She did not want to be too sleepy to work, and knew that wine in the middle of the day would make her sleepy. She didn't hurry the meal; she took her time, and finished with a little fresh fruit, followed by hot strong coffee from a vacuum jug.

Afterwards she pushed the table back into the hall of the suite, but the outer door was still locked, so she left it there and went back to work.

It was late afternoon before Ellis Lefèvre returned, and Claudia had almost finished her task. He paused in the doorway of the sitting-room to look at her, and she nerved herself to defy him, to force him to let her go home.

CHAPTER TWO

'I SEE you enjoyed your lunch—did I choose well?' Ellis Lefèvre asked, giving Claudia a mocking little smile, as though knowing she was poised on the edge of an explosion. He didn't wait for her to answer, but went on, 'I've put the table outside for room service to take away, I'll just ring them and ask them to bring up some tea. I'm very thirsty. I've been talking business endlessly and my throat is parched. Would you like some?'

'Oh...yes...thank you,' she said, temporarily disarmed by that light approach.

He picked up the phone and dialled room service's number, one hand in his jacket pocket jingling some keys or money, his long, slim body casually relaxed. Claudia tried to think of a polite but firm way of telling him she had to go home, but found it hard to concentrate because she was increasingly conscious of him. He might make her angry, but he was a very attractive man, and, even if she disliked what she knew of him so far, she couldn't help an instinctive reaction to the power of that masculinity.

Her eyes wandered over him. No, attractive wasn't quite the word to describe him. He wasn't handsome, or even good-looking. It was the conflict of opposites in the man that made the impact. That firm, cool mouth might be as tough as blazes, but it was sensual, too; no woman would miss the potential for passion in that full lower lip, and yet one felt that he was capable of icy control.

From under her lashes she watched him, wondering what might happen if that control ever snapped. She wouldn't like to be around if it did.

'Ah, room service,' he said coldly. 'I wondered if you were all dead. This is the Westmorland Suite. Yes, Mr Lefèvre. I would like tea for two, please, immediately—and will you remove the lunch table which is outside the suite doors?'

He hung up and came round behind her chair and she tensed as he bent over her shoulder to read the screen.

'How's your work coming?' His cheek lightly brushed her hair; she shifted slightly so that they no longer touched and felt his sideways glance, awareness and amusement in the look. He made no comment, merely said, 'You're doing well. You should finish in half an hour, then?'

'About that,' she agreed, assessing how much she still had to do.

He leaned on her desk with one hand and turned his body gracefully so that he could watch her, his grey eyes gleaming like polished silver.

Their faces were only inches apart. Claudia tried hard not to react to the way he watched her; she knew instinctively that he was taunting her, amusing himself by teasing her—perhaps because he knew she was trying not to be aware of him? His ego probably found that an unforgivable sin. She had only just met him, but one thing she was sure of—Ellis Lefèvre had a high opinion of himself, and expected others to have it, too.

She made herself start talking, to break up the disturbing intimacy he had deliberately set up. 'Mr Lefèvre, I really must go home tonight. I'm expected back at six and——'

'Who expects you?' he swiftly interrupted, the smile leaving his mouth and his eyes narrowing.

'My sister and brother-in-law—I told you, I live with them . . .'

'Over a restaurant, yes, I remember. What was it called?'

'Mirron's—it's not far from here, on the other side of St James's Park, it's quite successful now, although it was hard going for a while.' Pride glowed in her green eyes, because she felt as involved in the restaurant as Annette and Pierre were; she had worked hard, alongside them, over the past couple of years to help make Mirron's a success.

'Mirron's?' Ellis Lefèvre's brows contracted in thought. 'I think I know the place—small, intimate, a bistro type of restaurant? Parisian-style cooking? Mirron's—that's the name of the *patron*? Your brother-in-law?'

'Yes, Pierre Mirron,' she said, surprised and delighted that someone like Ellis Lefèvre should have heard of it. 'He's a wonderful chef; he trained in Paris at several of the top hotels before coming over to London.'

'Why did he come here? Because of your sister?'

'Oh, no, they only met here. Pierre came over to work for a year, just for the experience, intending to go back to France after that, but when he met Annette and married her he decided to stay in London.'

'She insisted on it?' he cynically suggested.

'Nothing of the kind!' Claudia said. 'In fact, I think Annette would love to live in France, but Pierre was convinced he would do better with his own restaurant over here. The struggle to get established in Paris is much harder. There's so much fierce competition. Also, I think Pierre likes living here.' She paused, re-

alising that he had managed to talk her miles off the
subject again, and frowned at him. 'Anyway, they're
expecting me back to help in the restaurant, you see—
I really must go at six.'

'Out of the question,' he said coolly, standing up
and walking away. 'Are you so stupid that you can't
understand a simple explanation? It is vital that you
should not talk to anybody until I have made my
speech, and until then you must stay here in this suite.
I'm sorry if it inconveniences you, but, I assure you,
you will be compensated. Generously compensated.
A bonus, I suggest? How much do you normally earn
for a day's work? I'll quadruple it.'

Her mouth was open to argue, but the offer took
her by surprise. She stared, breathless and incredulous, her mouth still open. Ellis Lefèvre turned to
survey her and laughed shortly.

'I take it that you accept?'

Claudia moistened her lips, thinking hard. 'Well...
What exactly...? I mean, if I did stay up here all
night ... I wouldn't ... I mean ...'

He raised sardonic brows. 'I am not buying your
body, Miss Thorburn—just your silence.'

She went crimson, her eyes hating him. 'I didn't
mean that!'

'No?' he mocked, and he was right, of course. She
had meant that; she had been trying to think of some
discreet way of making it plain that she was not
spending the night with him, only in his suite.

If she spent the night here, that was. Oh, why was
she pretending? She knew she was going to accept.
Quadruple her usual payment for one day's work? A
bitter little knife stabbed at her—oh, it was so easy
for Ellis Lefèvre to offer her that money. He wouldn't
even miss it in his bank account. It was small change

to him. He had no conception of what it meant to her. He couldn't begin to understand the desperate juggling she had to do to make ends meet.

'There are three bedrooms in the suite,' he said briskly, walking away towards the sitting-room door. 'Come and see, you can choose which you prefer.'

Claudia followed him uncertainly. He gestured to one door, which stood open, showing an enormous, beautifully furnished bedroom with a four-poster bed in the middle of it. 'That's my room,' he casually told her and did not linger but walked on to the next door, which he opened, and then opened a door opposite that. The rooms revealed were not as large as the one Ellis occupied, but they were bigger than the room Claudia had in her sister's flat. 'All the rooms are comfortable,' Ellis said. 'Each has its own bathroom. I can't see why you shouldn't have a good time while you're here. I would want you to do some more work, once you've finished with the speech—a few notes, a few letters, nothing arduous, but apart from that you would be free to watch TV, listen to music, read—whatever you choose. It is only one night out of your life, after all.'

Claudia stood in the doorway of one of the rooms, deliberately choosing the one which was not next door to the room Ellis occupied. There was a key in the lock, and a bolt on the door, too.

'This looks nice,' she said, liking the pink and cream of the décor.

'Good, then that's settled,' Ellis said coolly. 'Now, could you get the speech finished and printed out so that I can study it and rewrite if necessary? And don't look so horrified. I don't intend to make sweeping changes, just correct any mistakes. It won't involve much work for you.'

The phone rang and he walked over to answer it. Claudia went back to her keyboard and continued keying in the speech. Ellis spoke in a low, quiet voice and she tried not to hear a word he said. She was giving all her attention to her work, but she was getting tired now; her back aching, her eyes weary from staring at the screen for so long. She was dying to have a bath, slip into a kimono and relax...

That was when it dawned on her. She didn't have any night clothes with her! She looked at Ellis as he put the phone down and turned away.

'It just occurred to me! I haven't a nightdress or...or anything...with me. I can't stay.'

Ellis stared at her, his mouth hard. 'Isn't there a shop in the foyer of the hotel? They probably sell nightgowns.'

'Yes, but I'd have to go down to buy one,' she triumphantly pointed out. 'And if I can go down to do that, I can go home.'

'Quite unnecessary,' he bit out. 'What size are you? I'll ring down and tell them to bring up a selection for you to try on!'

Aghast, Claudia said, 'No, you can't! Are you crazy? They know me, and what's more I know the girl who works there, she's the biggest gossip in the place, and she's spiteful, too. She'd be bound to think I was sleeping with you.'

He considered that, frowning. 'Yes, very probably. Very well, I'll get her to bring up a selection and leave them for approval, and she need never see you. You can go into your own room and stay there until she has gone.'

'Oh, it's absurd,' Claudia said, but he walked to the phone and picked it up. 'Put me through to the hotel shop,' he told the operator, then asked Claudia again, 'What size?'

She reluctantly told him, then forced herself back to work, yet couldn't help hearing Ellis curtly telling the hotel shop manageress to bring up a selection of nightwear and lingerie, in her size, to his suite.

'Colour?' he repeated, turning his head to eye Claudia thoughtfully. 'Oh, white... Maybe pale green... No, not pink, definitely not pink.'

Claudia winced. That would make the manageress think hard. What hair colour rarely looked good with pink? A lot of the staff would know that she was working up here. They knew she had red hair. What if they put two and two together, and came up with the wrong answer?

'Oh, and slippers,' he said. 'Mules, black or white? You know the sort I mean... Lacy, silky things.'

He was staring at Claudia's long, slim legs. She glared until he looked up to meet her angry eyes, but all he did was mouth, 'What size shoe?'

She snapped back the answer and looked at her screen. She had made three stupid mistakes in one line. She went back to it, her flushed face irritated, and retyped the sentence. She was coming to the final page now, thank heavens, but she had the uneasy feeling that finishing the speech might only be the beginning of her problems.

She had just completed the entire process and was clipping the pages of each copy of the speech together when somebody rang the front doorbell. Ellis Lefèvre was talking on the phone. Claudia stood up, gave him an uncertain look, and he nodded to her, then said into the phone, 'Sorry, James, I have to go now, I'll talk to you again later.'

Hanging up, he said to Claudia, 'Go into your bedroom!' and strode past her towards the front door. She ran into the room she had chosen and quietly closed and bolted the door, standing behind it, listening to the deep, curt tones of Ellis's voice.

'Come in, bring them all into the sitting-room,' he said. 'This way, please.'

'I'll wait and take back those you will not require, sir,' said a voice she recognised, and she could easily imagine the expression on Betty Lloyd's face—catty, excited, curious.

'No, just leave them all. I'll make sure any we don't want are returned to you. The rest can be charged to my bill here.'

'Oh. Certainly. I hope the lady likes . . .' The voices died away as they vanished into the sitting-room. Claudia waited, listening intently, and after a moment or two heard them coming back.

'Well, thank you,' said Ellis, and there was a rustle of paper, then Betty Lloyd said, 'Oh, thank you, sir...' How big a tip had he given her? wondered Claudia. From the note in her voice, a very large tip indeed. She had rarely heard Betty sound so pleasant.

Ellis said, 'Good evening,' and the outer door of the suite closed. Claudia did not yet emerge; she wanted to be quite sure Betty Lloyd had gone. She heard Ellis's muted footsteps on the carpet. He tapped sharply on her door, making her jump.

'You can come out now! She's gone.'

She unbolted the door and opened it. He was already walking away; she followed him into the sitting-room and found him opening a square gold-printed box, shaking out of it an exquisite drift of cream lace and silk; he opened another box, which

held a delicate pastel-green nightie, began opening a
third, but Claudia stopped him.

'No, don't open them all! I only need one, and any
of them is fine!'

He gave her a sideways, glinting look. 'Aren't you
going to give me a fashion show?'

She stiffened, snatched up the cream nightdress and
walked away with it. 'I'll take this one! The rest can
go back.'

'Oh, I think you'll need these,' he said, holding out
another box.

She took it, saw that it was a matching set of
underwear in the same shade and style; slip, bra,
panties. Claudia had never been able to afford lingerie of that quality or price, and she couldn't resist
accepting these. After all, she told herself defiantly,
it was Ellis Lefèvre's fault that she had to stay here
overnight. She wouldn't need these things if she
weren't imprisoned here.

'Thank you,' she said, not meeting his amused gaze,
however, and took both boxes into her bedroom,
placing them on a chest of drawers. She stayed in there
for several minutes, reviewing her situation and feeling
distinctly worried. She did not like the way he had
asked if she was going to give him a fashion show.
Could she trust him? She looked at her watch, her
brows knitted. She would tell him she was very tired,
ask for an early supper to be sent up, eat it, and then
go to bed. No doubt he would be going down to dinner
with the other conference members; he wouldn't be
back for hours, and she would make quite sure that
her door was locked and bolted. She would not be
opening it, either, whatever he said.

She went back to the sitting-room and found Ellis
sitting behind the desk, his dark head bent, reading

a copy of the speech. She watched him skim down
the lines and was astonished by the speed with which
he went through each page. Now and then he would
halt, pick up a pen and make some small alteration,
so he must really be reading each word—but so fast
that she hardly believed it possible. He took no notice
of her, so she quietly finished clipping the other copies
and placing each in a prepared folder. She didn't look
at Ellis again, yet her senses were attuned to his every
movement: the calm, regular breathing, the rustle as
each page was turned, the long, sinewy hands holding
the speech, the very male body leaning back in the
chair, at ease and yet somehow always poised for
action. Claudia couldn't remember ever feeling this
aware of a man; it was a physical thing, a response
to him deep inside her own body.

He read the last page and looked up. 'Yes, that's
more or less what I wanted, but I've made a few alter-
ations—would you get those pages changed and
printed out again?'

He got up and walked out without waiting for her
to answer. Almost in disbelief she heard the outer door
close behind him as she hurriedly picked up the speech
and began flicking through the pages, noting every
change. Six ... no, seven ... Seven pages would have
to be altered and printed out again!

Rage burnt inside her. That would take her another
hour, even on the computer. She looked down at a
page—the alteration was so small, a change of phrase,
nothing more. Did he have to do that? It had sounded
fine the way it was—why change it? Oh, it might actually be better put this new way, but in her opinion
it was just a pointless waste of her time. That wouldn't
bother Ellis Lefèvre, of course. He had her penned

up here, a prisoner, with time on her hands, so why not make her work?

She cleared the desk again and sat down grimly to work as fast as she could. The telephone kept ringing. She was briskly polite and got rid of each new caller with as few words as possible, made a note of the name and time, and any message, then went back to work.

At last she reached the end of the revisions and once more clipped the pages of each copy together and slid them into their folders, sat back and closed her eyes, feeling exhausted.

She had felt tired when she got up this morning, she would much rather have stayed in bed—but she had come to work because she desperately needed the money, and her day had been one of the most hectic and trying of her whole life. She yawned and stretched. She was dying for another cup of tea, too. But she couldn't ring room service, because Ellis Lefèvre had the only key, and they would not be able to get in here until he returned. She looked at her watch. It was gone seven. How much longer would he be?

Surely he hadn't forgotten her and gone off to dinner with someone? She wouldn't be surprised if he had. That would be typical. Leaving her stranded here, without any food, while he talked business, ate a wildly expensive dinner and drank an even more expensive wine, no doubt!

And what was she supposed to do while she waited? Furiously, she got up and went into the room she had chosen, locked the door, picked up the nightdress and underwear that had been sent up from the shop, and tried them all on, at her leisure. The warm cream shade looked terrific against her red-gold hair; it was perfect for her colouring and gave her skin a wonderful glow. The négligé had a deep collar of lace, like a soft ruff, and floated around her, the feel of the wild silk on her skin so blissful that she kept both nightdress and négligé on while she switched on the television and curled up on the bed to watch a nature programme.

It was a mistake to lie down. She meant to dress again as soon as she heard Ellis Lefèvre return, but within ten minutes she was fast asleep, dreaming chaotically of everything that had happened that day, but in so jumbled a form that it took on the aspect of a nightmare. Someone was chasing her through a dark hotel, from strange room to strange room; terrified, she hid in a cupboard, but somebody knocked on the door and whispered her name. Claudia didn't dare move; she listened, trembling, and heard whoever was outside trying to open the door. No! she thought, horrified...

And then she woke up, hot and perspiring, a cry of panic on her lips, to sit up in total disarray, looking around the strange bedroom in shock, not knowing where she was or what had happened. For a second she thought she was still dreaming. Someone was knocking on the door. 'Claudia!' a deep voice impatiently said, and she stared at the door, petrified, then suddenly realised she was awake, remembered everything and knew that that was Ellis Lefèvre outside. He had come back at last.

Huskily, she called, 'I won't be a moment!' and slid off the bed, so unsteady that she fell and knocked over a gilt bedroom chair which fell with a crash.

'Are you OK?' Ellis said sharply.

'Yes,' she said, very flustered, getting to her feet and picking up the chair.

'Open this door!' Ellis demanded. 'Have you had an accident?'

'No...well...I just knocked over a chair... Please, I'll be out in a little while,' she wailed, wishing he would move away.

'You sound very odd,' he slowly said. 'Open the door now, let me see you——'

'No!' she cried in panic, grabbing at her own clothes and in her hurry managing to drop one of her shoes on her bare foot. She gave a little yelp.

'That's it! Open this door or I'll break it down!' Ellis snarled, hammering on the wooden panels, and Claudia was afraid he might actually manage to do it, so she pulled back the bolt and turned the key, backing away, clutching her clothes to her breast, as the door swung open and he charged through it.

He halted, his grey eyes flickering over her, then flashed a look around the room.

'There's nothing wrong, you see!' she told him defiantly. 'I was asleep when you knocked, that's all. Now, can I get dressed? And would you kindly order my dinner, because I'm starving and I want to eat and go to bed early?'

He nodded, coolly allowing his gaze to wander up and down her slender body in the creamy silk and lace. Claudia felt her nerve-ends prickle, her skin heating; she moved hurriedly to the door and pointedly held it open.

'I won't take long,' she said coldly.

He took two steps and was suddenly far too close. She froze as he fingered the deep lace collar of the négligé. 'You look very beautiful,' he said softly, and then before she had notice of his intention he had snatched her own clothes away from her and thrown them back on to the tumbled bed.

'What do you think you're doing?' Claudia tried to get away but he caught her hands and held her in an unbreakable grip.

'Don't bother to dress again,' he drawled. 'I prefer you that way. That boring grey outfit doesn't suit you at all; it makes you look prim and proper, a sort of grown-up schoolgirl.' His insolent gaze ran over her again and she became intensely conscious of the sensuality of his mouth; a look matched by the gleam in the grey eyes. 'But these make you look very different,' he murmured. 'Ravishing, very sexy...'

Claudia's breath caught for a second; her green eyes stared up at him, wide and disturbed.

For a second she felt distinctly odd; feverish, dizzy, as though she had the influenza which was sweeping through the hotel staff—and perhaps she did, she thought, almost with relief, because what else could explain the peculiar sensations? She hardly knew Ellis Lefèvre; he couldn't be causing her symptoms.

She pulled free and backed. 'Don't flirt with me, Mr Lefèvre! You promised me I needn't feel uneasy about spending the night in this suite; please keep your word, or I shall ring the hotel management and insist that someone comes up here to let me out!'

He pushed his hands into his pockets and made a wry face. 'I was paying you a compliment. What's wrong with that?'

Coldly, she said, 'You know very well what's wrong—I don't want your compliments, I don't want you flirting with me. I'm here simply and solely to work for you as a secretary. If you want a woman for some other purpose, I suggest you look around Soho.'

He didn't like that and his grey eyes flashed in temper, as bright as white-hot steel. Claudia pretended he didn't make her nervous, looking at her

that way. She said coldly, 'Now, I want to get
dressed—would you leave my room, please?'

He bared his teeth at her in a mock smile. 'Very
well. Any preferences?'

'What?' She stiffened, ready to lose her temper
again, and he gave her a coolly mocking look.

'About dinner?'

'Oh,' she said, and he smiled like a duellist who
had drawn blood.

'Do you want to read the room service menu,' he
softly asked, 'or have you already got something in
mind?'

She had the definite feeling that he was talking on
two levels, playing games with her, having fun at her
expense, but she was not going to encourage him.

'I'll be happy with a salad,' she said calmly. 'And
I would like to eat soon—so could you ring down right
away?'

He bowed and left, and Claudia bolted the door
behind him with a stifled sigh of relief. It was becoming an ordeal being with the man.

She looked at her watch and realised with a shock
that she hadn't rung Annette to warn her that she
wouldn't be home, so she hurriedly picked up the
phone and got an outside line.

'Not coming home tonight?' Annette sounded
startled. 'Claudia, what are you up to? I know I told
you to start having fun, but I wasn't expecting you
to take me at my word!' She giggled. Claudia didn't,
remembering that this conversation was being recorded and would be heard by Ellis Lefèvre later.

'I'm having to stay on to work, or rather to be on
call, in case I do have to work,' she said flatly. 'It
isn't worth coming home later, so I'm staying in the

hotel, but if you want me you can ring me on extension 453.'

'Where's that? A cupboard up in the attics?' Annette knew that if staff did live in at the hotel they were always given the very worst of the rooms, the one guests would complain about.

Claudia let her eyes wander around the elegant bedroom, her face ironic. 'Not quite,' she said drily. 'I must go, Annette. See you some time tomorrow. Sorry I can't help in the restaurant tonight. I hope you don't have too hectic an evening.'

'We'll manage,' Annette assured her. 'I hope you won't have to work at all; maybe you can get an early night for once, and get up late.'

'Maybe,' Claudia said.

She hung up and dressed again in her grey suit and white blouse, brushed her hair and did her make-up. The mirror showed her a neat, reserved, remote young woman; it was the image she wanted tonight. She did not want Ellis Lefèvre to have any wrong ideas about her. Obviously he was a flirt, and Claudia had no intention of becoming one of the scalps dangling from his belt. She couldn't deny she found him interesting; that switch from a hard, icy businessman who had himself very much under control to a teasing, mocking charmer was a fascinating one, but not contradictory. The man who could bulldoze a company into accepting a merger they had never sought was very much the same man as the one who had been making advances to her just now. The technique wasn't identical, but the ruthless, unscrupulous nature of the man was the same. He might chase her, but she was not going to let him catch her.

When she emerged there was no sign of him, however. His bedroom door was closed; she listened outside it and heard him whistling, heard the sound of a shower running. She went back into the sitting-room and turned on the television, curled up in a corner of the couch and watched a documentary on Egypt for twenty minutes, fascinated by the contrasts between the ancient civilisation of the countryside and the modern streets of Cairo.

The programme was just ending when Ellis Lefèvre reappeared. He was in immaculate evening dress: black jacket and trousers, a pleated white shirt and black bow tie, his hair smooth and gleaming. He stood in the doorway, inspecting her with derision.

'Your meal should be up here any moment,' he said. 'I'll stay to make sure you get it, then I'm off downstairs to dinner.'

'How nice for you,' Claudia said bitingly. 'Do enjoy yourself.'

He laughed. 'Why, thank you, I intend to.'

Room service arrived at that second; he went to unlock the door and dismissed the waiter at once. Claudia watched Ellis wheel the table into the sitting-room. No doubt he would be eating a first-rate cordon bleu meal while she was tucking into her salad. She knew that the cabaret after dinner downstairs was very entertaining at the moment; the female singer was supposed to be brilliant. The conference guests would sit through that and then dance the night away. Weren't they lucky? All she had to look forward to was an early night.

Ellis was watching her as he placed a chair in front of the table. 'You look wistful—sure you don't want me to stay?'

Her chin went up and she gave him an irritated look. 'Quite sure, thank you!'

He shrugged. 'Well, goodnight, then. Sleep well and don't dream, will you? But I'm sure you won't.'

Claudia bit back the angry retort she wanted to throw at his departing figure. He thought he was so funny! Well, she didn't. She heard the suite door close and sat down in front of the table. He hadn't ordered her a salad at all. He had chosen a very different meal for her, and she explored the various dishes eagerly.

To begin with, black pearls of caviare on crushed ice, served in a silver goblet, and garnished with chopped boiled egg and chopped raw onion and parsley. To follow that, thinly sliced breast of chicken with a delicate mushroom sauce, mangetout peas, a tomato and basil salad, and spears of asparagus which must have been flown from the other side of the world. The sweet was a peach and mango sorbet, and was delicious.

It was too good to hurry, and afterwards while she drank her coffee she watched television, a very funny play by Alan Ayckbourn, which she had missed when it was on in London the previous year. It was half-past ten before she was actually in bed, but by then she was so relaxed that she fell asleep at once.

The phone woke her abruptly. For a moment she lay dazedly listening to it, then realising that nobody else was going to answer it, she did, sleepily, stifling a yawn. 'Yes? Hello?'

There was a silence, then an icy voice said, 'Who is that?'

Claudia was sure she knew the voice and stupidly dithered. 'Er—I'm——' she mumbled.

The caller snapped, 'Oh, never mind, I know who you are! I never forget a voice or a face. Tell him I want to talk to him!' Her tone was ominous.

Claudia knew who *she* was, too. She had recognised Estelle's voice almost at once, and got a certain kick out of saying politely, 'I'm sorry, Mr Lefèvre isn't available at the moment.'

'I suppose the pair of you are in bed!' Estelle accused furiously. 'Did he tell you to get rid of whoever was on the phone? Never mind, don't bother to lie. I'll talk to him tomorrow, I don't want to talk to him now, not if he's with you. Oh, I knew you had your eye on him, the minute I set eyes on you. I wasn't born yesterday; I've seen your sort before. Little two-bit secretaries with an eye on the boss...but you don't worry me. I know him. He'll get bored with you once he's had you. He always does. He has a very low boredom threshold. So don't get ambitious, because you haven't got a hope. You're just a one-night stand; enjoy it while it lasts.'

The slam of the phone made Claudia almost deaf for several minutes.

She hung up, too, flushed and furious, hearing the insults, repeating over and over again in her head, like a gramophone record that had stuck in one groove. She wished she had managed to say something, tell the other woman what she thought of her, but she had been too aghast.

Now she lay awake in the dark, obsessively going over what Estelle had said. The woman had a poisonous mind—but she had been telling the truth in what she said about Ellis. That pass he had made earlier made that obvious. Estelle had been wrong in guessing that Claudia was in bed with him, but if Claudia hadn't turned him down she might so easily have been dead accurate. It made Claudia shudder to imagine what could have been happening when Estelle rang.

Where was he now, anyway? With some more available woman? Claudia rolled over and looked at the clock. Midnight. Well, he wasn't talking business at this hour, surely? Estelle made late phone calls. But then, maybe she was often with Ellis Lefèvre at this hour. Presumably when he wasn't chasing someone new she was his bedfellow. How could she stand a relationship like that? Claudia grimaced in distaste. She wouldn't put up with a man who treated her that way; it must be so humiliating and painful. She might not like Estelle, but she felt sorry for her.

Turning over again, she made herself stop thinking about the whole messy situation, and fell asleep again soon afterwards. Ellis still hadn't returned by then, and yet when Claudia emerged from her bedroom next morning, freshly showered but still wearing her grey suit, she found Ellis in the sitting-room, reading the pink pages of the *Financial Times* while he ate his breakfast at a table by the window, the sunlight giving his smooth skin a golden gleam.

She eyed him coldly, thinking that he had no right to look that eye-catching after a night on the tiles. Or was that what gave his hair the glossy look, put the gleam in his eye?

He looked up and nodded to her. 'The coffee is in a vacuum jug, so it is still hot, and the croissants are delicious. If you want a cooked breakfast, ring down for one.'

'I am quite happy with croissants,' Claudia said offhandedly, and he gave her a dry look.

'I see you slept well and have got up in your usual cheerful mood.'

She sat down and poured herself some coffee, ignoring that. He watched her, his mouth hostile, then swallowed the last of his coffee, folded his newspaper, and got to his feet.

'I shall be making my speech at eleven, so you may leave the suite any time after that, but please stay in here until then, and take any calls.'

'Yes, sir,' she said in the same remote voice, spreading black cherry jam on a croissant without even looking at him.

'Oh, to hell with you, I'm not hanging around here playing the *Titanic* to your iceberg,' Ellis bit out, and left, banging the door of the suite as he left, and she slackened, looking at her croissant without real interest. She drank some coffee and then abandoned the idea of breakfast. It must be shortage of sleep that made her feel low in spirits.

She took a string of calls for Ellis over the next couple of hours, and made copious notes for him, which she left on the desk. Just after eleven she rang down to the secretarial office and Judy Smith cheerfully told her that several of the girls had come back from sick leave.

'You've been on duty for twenty-four hours now, so you had better take a day off and I'll replace you with Marianne Edwards. She's very experienced.'

'She'll need to be,' Claudia said bitterly. 'I'm locked in here, though—Ellis Lefèvre has the key.'

'No, he left one with me so that I could let you out,' Judy said complacently. 'I'll send it up with Marianne, then you can go home, lovie.'

A few minutes later, Marianne arrived and Claudia handed over to her, leaving the boxed lingerie and nightwear in Ellis Lefèvre's room. She took with her the ones she had used. She had earned them, in her opinion. Would he pay her that bonus? she wondered. Or would he conveniently forget his promise?

Next day she found out. Judy Smith rang her, sounding embarrassed and apologetic. 'Darling, I'm really very sorry about this, I hate doing it, but I'm not being given the option, I have to do it...'

'Do what?' Claudia asked, frowning.

'I've been told to fire you,' said Judy.

CHAPTER THREE

'THEY can't do that!' Annette said indignantly, her deft hands busy chopping carrots while she talked. 'Not these days. If you fire anyone without a good reason you're in trouble. You can take them to court, get compensation, you know!'

Claudia was sorting through a basket of mushrooms which had just arrived from the market. 'I wasn't on the permanent staff, Annette. I was just a part-time worker; I wanted to be free to work as and when I pleased, but that means I can't complain if they tell me they don't want me any more.'

'I don't see why, unless they have a good reason. What exactly did Judy say?'

'Just that she had been told to get rid of me.' Claudia washed and dried her hands and began to wash the cabbages before preparing them.

'Who by? Didn't she say?' Annette had piled a mountain of sliced carrots up on her board and now she pushed them all into a great bowl of iced water.

'The hotel manager gave the order, but Judy says it was Ellis Lefèvre who wanted me fired.' Claudia's eyes glittered with temper. 'I didn't have a very high opinion of the man, but I must say I didn't think even he would stoop this low—making sure I lost my job just because——' She broke off and her sister turned to stare, her face curious.

'Just because...?' Her eyes searched Claudia's flushed face and then she began to laugh. 'Oh, no! He didn't make a pass? That rich Swiss you were

48

working for?' Claudia didn't smile back, and Annette
stopped laughing and looked angry. 'You're serious.
What is all this? Was that why...? Claudia! Was that
why you stayed at the hotel overnight? What has been
going on at that place? Were you forced to stay? I
thought you sounded odd when you rang up—was
this guy Le...whatever his name is...was he with
you? Did he make you...? What did he do to you,
Claudia?' Annette dried her hands and put both arms
around her sister, hugging her. 'Tell me, you can tell
me... I'm on your side, you know that. Whatever
happened, we'll deal with it.'

Claudia was appalled; her sister had gone too fast
and too far, and she was crimson to her hairline. 'No,
it wasn't like that,' she muttered, wishing she hadn't
told Annette why she was leaving the hotel. The very
idea that her sister believed she had spent last night
in bed with Ellis Lefèvre made her want to hide somewhere. 'He didn't... I mean, nothing happened...
Not what you mean, anyway. Well, not really.'

Her incoherence and look of horror made Annette
even more sympathetic. 'You poor girl,' she said.
'Don't be embarrassed, nobody is going to blame you.
Men like that make me sick. Who does he think he
is? It's the money, you know—makes them think they
own the earth, can do just as they like. Well, he's
going to learn he can't!'

'Annette, stop it!' Claudia burst out, pushing her
away and shaking her head at her. 'You don't understand. I didn't spend the night with him, just in his
suite, because I'd typed this confidential speech—I
told you... It was just that... Oh, he made a pass,
but nothing serious—he was only trying it on, and I
slapped him down, that's all. He didn't like it, but he
left, in a temper, and——'

'So he got you fired!' Annette was fiercely incredulous, getting as upset about it as if it had happened to her. 'How utterly typical. That's sexual harassment, and you can definitely get him on that. I tell you what, you remember that guy in the really old, dirty jeans who comes in here on a Saturday night and leers at you over his *coq au vin*?'

Claudia stared, completely lost now. 'What? Well, yes, I suppose so... What on earth has he got to do with this?'

'He's a lawyer, he'll tell you how to get compensation,' Annette triumphantly concluded, and Claudia's jaw dropped.

'A lawyer? Him? But he never even shaves.'

'He shaves on weekdays,' Annette assured her. 'He came in here the other day at lunchtime with one of his clients, wearing a suit. A good one, too, really well cut. He looked totally different, and I overheard enough to realise he was a lawyer. He paid and I asked him outright, and he admitted it. He said he takes the weekends off for bad behaviour.'

Claudia had to laugh at that, then she sobered. 'All the same, I can't ask him for free advice—it isn't fair. You wouldn't like it if he asked for a free meal, would you?'

'We could do a swap, though,' suggested Annette. 'A few free dinners for an hour's consultation?'

Laughing again, Claudia shook her head. 'No, thanks. I'm going in tomorrow to see Judy about any money I'm owed; I'll tell her I'm thinking of suing the hotel and see where that gets me. They may offer me compensation. I'll talk to the agency this afternoon and ask their advice. If I am entitled to any money from the hotel, they'll know.'

'Yes, that's true,' agreed Annette and that afternoon Claudia took the bus up to Oxford Street to see the manageress of the employment agency who had got her the hotel job.

'They have to give you a reason for firing you,' she was told. 'I'll ring and ask them. Hang on.'

She dialled the hotel's number and asked for Judy Smith. 'Hello, Jenny Newton here—I gather you have let Claudia Thorburn go. Can you tell me why? I thought you were quite satisfied with her work.' She listened, frowning, doing doodles on a pad in front of her.

Claudia waited tensely, wishing she could hear what Judy was saying.

'That doesn't sound like her,' Jenny said slowly. 'What did he mean, insolent? Sure she didn't have provocation? Oh, come on, Judy, you know what I mean very well. Some men think a temp is a soft target and if she turns them down they can get very nasty.' She listened, again, chewing her lower lip. 'Yes, hard to prove either way. How long is he staying for? Couldn't you give her a week off and then take her back once he has gone?'

There was a brief silence again, then she grimaced. 'I see—the management won't take her back? Well, we'll have to reserve our position, but I feel bound to say I think she is entitled to compensation. I'll talk to you later after I've consulted my client.'

Jenny put the phone down and looked across the desk at Claudia. 'Sorry, they...'

'I heard. Thanks for trying. What do you think my chances are of getting compensation?'

'Fair, but it won't be much because you were just a casual worker. You might get an extra week's wages.

The trouble is, you can't prove you weren't insolent
to the man——'

'I wish I'd been a damn sight more insolent!'
Claudia muttered, and Jenny smiled ruefully.

'I know how you feel, and if you had any evidence
to support your allegation I'd back you to the hilt,
but as it is ... It's just your word against his, and he
has all the clout.' She pulled open her card index and
began flicking through it. 'Well, meanwhile, let's see
what we can find for you ...'

She found several jobs, and rang the firms, managing to get Claudia two interviews to go to next day.
'The money won't be as good,' she warned. 'But they
are flexible about hours.'

Annette was scathing when Claudia told her what
had happened. 'So the fact is, this wonderful agency
isn't going to back you at all. She went through the
motions but when the hotel stood by the decision she
accepted it without a fight.'

'What could she do?' Claudia shrugged impatiently. 'She's right—it is my word against his.
Look, drop it, Annette. I can't be bothered to waste
any more time on it. The job wasn't that important
to me.'

Her sister was far more belligerent and always had
been; she smouldered on and off for the rest of the
day and was still furious when they began serving
dinner to a crowded restaurant.

Claudia was carrying a loaded tray out to the
kitchen when she saw some newcomers making their
way to an empty table. She froze in her tracks, almost
dropping the tray, the glasses on it rattling as her hands
shook. An angry flush rushed up her face, then she
hurried through the swing doors and dumped her tray.

Annette was taking a cheese soufflé out of the oven very gently and growled at her, 'Don't make a draught near this or it will sink, and then I'll kill you.'

'He's in there,' Claudia stammered. 'How he has the nerve! Walking in here as bold as brass... I nearly threw my tray at him...'

Annette wasn't really listening; she was giving all her attention to the delicately risen soufflé which she was placing on a tray. 'Take this in at once,' she said. 'Hurry, or it will be ruined.'

Pierre was yelling over his stoves. 'Truffle... Where's the chopped truffle?'

They were too busy to listen, realised Claudia, obediently taking the soufflé from her sister. She took a deep breath, then went back into the restaurant, keeping her eyes away from the part of the room where Ellis Lefèvre sat with his guest. She still managed to notice that it was a man with him; younger, very thin, with a pale complexion and dull brown hair. Was it one of his executives?

They were not sitting at one of Claudia's tables, thank heavens, so she might never need to confront Ellis. She went back into the kitchen to collect another table's main course, and was caught by Annette as soon as she reappeared.

'What did you say just now?' Annette was very flushed, her eyes fiery. 'You didn't say that that man is here, in the restaurant, did you?'

'At table three,' Claudia said, checking the waiting meals. She picked up the plates meant for her clients and turned to hurry back, almost bumping into Annette who was peering through the small window in the swing door.

'Which one?' Annette demanded, eyes like a gimlet, and Claudia gave her an incredulous look. Surely that was obvious? By no stretch of the imagination could anyone describe the younger man as sexy and disturbingly attractive. She bit her lip self-consciously—but then she hadn't ever told Annette what Ellis Lefèvre was like, had she? In fact, she had carefully avoided telling Annette anything much about him at all.

'Well, he's not the skinny, pallid one,' she said drily, and went back into the restaurant. She rigidly kept her gaze away from Ellis, yet she knew that he was watching her. She could feel his eyes like the heat of a fire, and their scrutiny made her nerves leap.

What was he doing here? He had got her sacked, and yet here he was tonight, staring at her, willing her to look his way, almost as though he was trying to hypnotise her. What did he want? She winced. Well, she knew that. But why was he here tonight? What was he after? Did he hope that she would be more amenable now that she had discovered what damage he could do her? Had he complained about her to the hotel to show her just how influential he was, how much weight he carried with her employers?

She hurried back into the kitchen again and found her sister slamming steak over the charcoal grill in the corner, muttering furiously to herself about Ellis Lefèvre. 'We don't want him here; tell him to go, chuck him out, I'm not feeding him, unless it's with arsenic!'

'*Chérie*, we can't throw him out,' Pierre shouted over the sizzle of his pans. 'It would cause a scene, and we cannot have scenes in the restaurant, we would lose customers. So we don't like him? So OK. *Tant pis*. But we cook superbly for him, for everyone, because it is our reputation and we must never drop our standards. Cooking is like the theatre. The show must go on, yes?'

'No,' Annette yelled back. She turned to look at Claudia. 'You don't have to go back in there, with that man around. I'll take over your tables.'

'Ellis Lefèvre doesn't bother me!' Claudia said and Annette gasped, mouth wide open, which Claudia felt was a little over the top as a reaction. So it wasn't strictly true that Ellis did not bother her? So she was pretending—and it showed a little? Annette didn't have to make such a meal of her incredulity.

Annette made funny choky noises, jerking her head, and Claudia was quite anxious about her for a second until she suddenly caught on to the fact that her sister was trying to tell her something. But what? Only then did it dawn on her that Annette was staring past her at someone standing right behind her.

She swung round and felt her nerves jerk violently as she met Ellis Lefèvre's cool grey eyes.

'So I don't bother you?' he drawled.

'No,' Claudia bit out. 'You don't. And what are you doing in here, anyway? This kitchen is out of bounds to clients. Go back to your table and wait for your meal.' She paused, realised her sharp tone had been a little lacking in customer persuasion, and gave him a false, icy smile. 'Please, sir,' she added as if the words were knives she was hurling at him.

'I want to talk to you,' he merely said, and Annette made high-pitched, wordless comments, listening to them.

Claudia saw that any minute her sister was going to start hurling crockery at him. Annette was so angry she couldn't even say a word, which was a first for her. Annette usually had so much to say for herself.

The automatic dishwasher had spun to a stop and Claudia walked over to start unloading it, picking up a clean dishcloth.

'Anyone who comes into this kitchen is expected to work,' she told Ellis, offering him the cloth. 'Either help, or get out. We're too busy for social visits, we work for a living in here.'

He took the cloth automatically. 'Look, I realise you're angry——'

'Oh, he realises that!' Claudia said to Annette, while she opened the dishwasher and hot steam gushed out into the room, making Ellis jump back out of range. 'Isn't that sensitive of him? He has me fired, but he realises it has upset me! What a wonderful guy.'

'What did you say?' Ellis asked, automatically taking one of the hot plates and drying it. 'Had you fired? What are you talking about?'

'You know very well what I'm talking about—don't play dumb with me!'

Annette dried plates too, but much faster, her technique experienced.

'Are you talking about your job at the hotel?' Ellis was frowning, his grey eyes narrowed. 'You've been fired? When was this? They must have given a reason——'

'They told me the truth,' Claudia said coldly. 'They told me you had complained that I was insolent and were insisting that I must be dismissed. They said they were very sorry, but the hotel can't afford to offend a guest as important as you, so I was given my cards.' She eyed him contemptuously. 'And don't try lying to me, because it won't work. I know what your game is, Mr Lefèvre! You think you have the advantage now I've lost my job. You think I'll have to agree to your terms, dance to your tune—well, I won't and nothing will ever make me. If I never see you again, it will be too soon for me.'

He put down the dishcloth, his lean face very serious. 'Claudia, I swear to you, I had nothing whatever to do with your dismissal. I never complained about you, I certainly didn't want to get you fired. I don't know what did really happen, but I assure you I'll find out, and have you reinstated, and given an apology.'

'Take no notice of him, Claudia!' Annette erupted, her face highly flushed. 'He's lying through his teeth.'

Ellis ignored her, his grey eyes intent on Claudia, who was staring at him uncertainly. He managed somehow to be convincing, she half believed him, but why would Judy lie?

'Just go away,' Claudia told him. 'I don't believe you.'

'Neither do I,' Annette said. They both ignored her. Pierre yelled, 'Is anybody working in here, or am I running this restaurant on my own?' Annette rushed away with a little wail.

Ellis went on staring at Claudia. 'I didn't know you had been fired; I was simply told you weren't at work. I assumed you were taking time off, I thought you were staying away from the hotel because of me, so I came looking for you.'

'Why?' she asked huskily, then her colour darkened, and she said sharply, 'No, don't tell me, I don't want to know, I just want you to go away and never come back. You've done me enough damage as it is— whether it was you who actually got me fired or your girlfriend.'

'Estelle,' he thought aloud, frowning. 'Yes, it must have been Estelle, of course.' He grimaced. 'Well, if it was her then I'm afraid there isn't much chance that I'll be able to get you reinstated——'

'I never thought there was!' she bitterly told him. 'It's still your fault, even if you didn't actually complain about me. If you hadn't flirted with me and kept me in your suite all night, your girlfriend wouldn't have got jealous and wouldn't have fired me.'

'OK, I accept that. Let me make amends, then. You haven't found another job yet, have you?' He paused, watching her, reading her expression. 'No? Good. Then come and work for me. My personal secretary is leaving soon, to get married—the salary is far better than you must have earned in the hotel.' He named a figure that took her breath away and she drew a sharp, startled breath. 'You would be travelling quite often, all over the world,' Ellis said softly. 'The company would provide a luxury flat, a car, and pay all your expenses.'

Annette was listening again, her eyes like saucers, while she automatically stirred the sauce she was helping Pierre to make.

Claudia couldn't believe her ears. It was too good to be true—a magnificent offer, the sort of job any girl would give her eye-teeth to get. She couldn't think what to say for a moment. She looked helplessly at her sister, signalling with her eyes, and Annette shrugged her shoulders, making it clear she didn't know what to think, either. Claudia looked back at Ellis, who gave her a curling smile, raising his dark brows.

'Don't tell me that for once I've taken your breath away?'

Claudia stiffened, suddenly seeing satisfaction in those grey eyes, a complacency in the curve of his mouth. He looked altogether too pleased with himself.

Her suspicion flared again—had he, after all, been responsible for getting her fired? Had that been part of a devious plan, intended to make her vulnerable to an offer of a job with him? She thought his offer over again. A salary higher than she had ever in her wildest dreams imagined earning, a luxury flat, a car and a big expense account... and worldwide travel as Ellis Lefèvre's companion?

Her eyes widened and darkened with insult and fury. Oh, yes, it was too good to be true! She had been dumb, not to have seen through his generous offer at once. It was so blatant an idiot should have known what it really was.

Eyeing him contemptuously, she bit out, 'Secretary isn't quite the right job description, is it? No mere secretary, however high-powered, gets terms like that! Do you think I'm stupid? Well, I'm not, Mr Lefèvre. The answer is no. I don't want your money, or your company flat, or your car or the expense account. I won't become your mistress. Now, go away, before I get my brother-in-law to throw you out.'

He stared at her, pretending to be surprised, then said impatiently, 'Claudia, don't be ridiculous, just listen to me——'

One of the waitresses had just got a jug of cold watercress and cucumber soup out of the fridge and was about to ladle some into a soup bowl. Claudia snatched the jug from her, and, without stopping to think, threw it all over Ellis Lefèvre.

He gave a sharp gasp. Annette gave a shriek. Pierre broke into agitated French, moaning, *'Oh, mon Dieu, mon Dieu, ma soupe! Oh, ma soupe. Claudia, tu es foue...'*

Claudia was frozen on the spot, staring at Ellis, who stared back, his face running with the smooth green cream of the soup. Fragments of watercress showed here and there; a fleck had caught in his thick black lashes, and there were slivers of cucumber in his hair, on his collar, on the shoulders of his jacket.

It would have been a funny sight, if either of them had been in a mood to see the humour of it, but Claudia was too horrified by what she had done, and afraid of his reaction—and Ellis had apparently been turned to stone.

After what seemed to Claudia the longest moment of her life, he reached out and picked up the cloth he had been using and wiped his face and hair. Claudia picked up another cloth, beginning to brush his shirt and jacket clean, but he knocked her hand away, then turned on his heel and walked out without another word.

'Oh, dear!' Annette said inadequately, staring in disbelief at his vanishing figure before she turned her horrified eyes on her sister.

Pierre was standing there too, open-mouthed and apparently lost for words. Then there was a strong smell of burning and Pierre swore in violent French, snatching a pan, containing blackened *escalope de veau*, off the stove. He flung it, pan and all, into the kitchen waste-bin, then tore at his hair with both hands.

'First my soup, and now the *escalope*!' he shouted. 'What do you mean to ruin next, Claudia? Why don't you just cut my throat and get it over with quickly. What do I tell my customers, eh? Maybe you like to go out there and pour soup over all of them?'

Claudia burst into tears and rushed out of the kitchen and up the back stairs to the flat she shared with her sister and brother-in-law. She shouldn't have thrown that soup over Ellis. Oh, he deserved it—she didn't regret throwing it at him. She was sorry she had used Pierre's special soup, though. No wonder Pierre was furious. She couldn't blame him. He was proud of his cold cress and cucumber soup; it was popular.

Pierre was temperamental, of course, but then a good chef often was—things were always going wrong in a kitchen. Even the best chefs made mistakes, and then they became angry or depressed, and brooded or broke things.

She knew Pierre would get over his rage; he would be sorry for shouting at her, once he had recovered his sense of humour, and she would apologise and promise not to chuck his soup over anyone again, Pierre would roar with laughter, and then they would be friends again.

Ellis was another matter. Ellis had insulted her. What did he think she was? She burned with indignation every time she thought about that offer, but inexplicably she was unable to stop herself crying, either, and spent ten minutes on her bed, her face buried in the quilt, occasionally kicking her bed in a fury, as if she wished it were Ellis Lefèvre.

It must have been more than an hour later that Annette came up to knock at her door. 'Come on, love, open up, let me talk to you!'

Claudia by then had splashed cold water on her face, brushed out her hair, straightened her dress, and was sitting in a chair by the window staring out at the London street lights and above them the plum-dark London night sky which reflected them.

She was quiet and sober now. She unlocked her door and Annette came in, warily eyeing her face.

'I'm sorry for the scene,' Claudia said flatly.

'Don't be silly! We don't blame you.'

'I lost my tempter. I didn't stop to think ... I felt awful about Pierre's lovely soup, what a waste...'

Annette gave a sudden giggle. 'Oh, but he looked so funny... like someone who has been fished out of a pond, covered in green slime...'

'Yes,' said Claudia, quite struck, 'That's just how he looked!' She thought about the scene, Ellis standing there, his eyes metallic and icy, and then she groaned, 'Oh, he was so furious!'

'Serves him right!' Annette sturdily said. 'Imagine it—asking you to be his mistress! Well! The nerve of the man! For a minute I didn't catch on, I was so flabbergasted by the money he talked about, by all the wonderful perks... but, of course, when you accused him and I saw his face, then I knew you were right. That was what he meant, all right.' Annette's teeth met and she reddened with temper. 'And of course Pierre thought it very funny.'

'Is he still angry with me? Not that I'd blame him, if he is!'

'No, don't worry. He's back to normal now. We've finished serving all the tables, the last customers are on their coffees, and Pierre is having his usual coffee and brandy. He did annoy me, though, saying that he saw nothing so very odd in that man's disgusting proposition. He said it was very rational, very French. Many Frenchmen have a mistress, especially when they're middle-aged and bored with their wives, Pierre said. I told him that if he was thinking of taking a mistress he had better think again because I'd be after him with a meat cleaver, if he did! He seemed quite flattered by that.'

Claudia laughed. 'He likes to think you're jealous, it soothes his ego.'

'Aren't men unbelievable?' Annette said. 'I pointed out to him that Ellis Lefèvre wasn't French, but Swiss, and Pierre said, yes, but he was from French-speaking Switzerland, which it seems is a wonderful thing to be, or so Pierre seemed to think. Couldn't be better, according to him. The Swiss are so rich, and speaking French too they are very civilised. And very correct, too, Pierre said, coming to make you the offer in front of your family—excellent terms, and there would have been a contract, all legally drawn up and some sort of severance pay on a sliding scale, according to how long you had been with him——'

'Stop it!' Claudia burst out, quite distraught, and her sister stopped obediently, looking at her anxiously.

'I was only joking, love!'

'He wasn't,' Claudia snapped. 'Ellis Lefèvre meant it. He was offering me a lot of money, and it wasn't for secretarial work, whatever he may have pretended.'

'No,' agreed Annette drily.

'Maybe I'm more old-fashioned than I thought I was—but I was insulted,' Claudia said. 'I bet he's never offered her money...'

'Her?' Annette looked confused.

'That Estelle girl, whose father is mixed up with the management of the hotel. Ellis Lefèvre wouldn't dream of trying to buy her! He might marry her one day, but me... Oh, I'm nobody—I'm just a secretary, without money or influence. Men like Ellis Lefèvre don't marry girls like me!'

'Claudia, you only met him a couple of days ago,' her sister slowly reminded her. 'You surely can't be taking him seriously? What went on in that suite at the hotel, for heaven's sake?'

'Nothing! Nothing at all!' Claudia said, forcing herself to meet Annette's eyes without flinching or looking away. She saw relief in her sister's face. She had managed to convince Annette. It wasn't so easy to convince herself.

Next day she had an interview for a part-time job in an accountant's office, but knew almost from the start that she hadn't got a hope of succeeding. The thin, middle-aged woman behind the desk kept looking at her red-gold hair, big green eyes and slender figure, and pursing her lips in disapproval.

'I don't think you are really suitable,' she told her at last. 'I don't feel you would fit in here.'

Claudia didn't feel she would, either. She walked back to the restaurant, to save money, wondering how long her savings would last if she didn't get another job soon. She had to pay her voice coach and her dance studio, on Wednesday she had an audition out in the wilds of a North London suburb and she needed new shoes.

The hotel job had been the best she had ever had. Varied, interesting, enjoyable—until she had met Ellis Lefèvre!

She walked round to the back of the restaurant to go in through the kitchen entrance, but just before she reached the door a young man got out of a parked car, stepped into her path and gave her a shy, uneasy smile.

'Miss Thorburn? Hello, you probably don't remember me—I was here last night, with my brother...'

Claudia looked blankly at him for a second, then suddenly recognised his pale complexion, the thin, serious face and brown hair and eyes. It was the young man who had been in the restaurant with Ellis last night.

'Brother?' she repeated, taken aback. Surely not? There was no resemblance to Ellis whatsoever.

'Yes, I'm Stephen Lefèvre.' He politely offered his hand, but Claudia didn't take it. She was frowning, her green eyes alive with suspicion and hostility.

'What do you want here, Mr Lefèvre?' she asked coldly. 'I thought I'd made myself quite clear to your brother? I don't want to set eyes on him again and I'm not interested in his proposition. Go back to him and tell him that I haven't changed my mind, nor will I.'

'He doesn't even know I'm here,' Stephen Lefèvre said quietly. 'I'm not here on his behalf, I assure you.'

She stared, wondering whether or not to believe him. 'Then what do you want?' she demanded.

'Ellis doesn't usually confide in me,' he said. 'But last night, he did tell me how you came to lose your job. He feels responsible——'

'He was responsible!' she angrily interrupted, then said quickly, 'Nevertheless, I don't want anything from him, so if you've come with another of his insulting suggestions——'

'I told you, he doesn't even know I'm here. This was all my idea, and it may be crazy, it may not work out, but somehow just from the look of you I felt maybe it could——'

'What are you talking about?' Claudia impatiently asked.

'I don't know if Ellis ever mentioned our father,' Stephen said, startling her.

She shook her head. 'I really barely know your brother; I know nothing whatever about your family.'

'Well, our father has been progressively going blind for several years, and he hasn't found it very easy to cope with... He's resentful and touchy, and... well, frankly, he has become damned difficult to live with. He's living just outside London, in a house on the

Thames. He's writing a book, which means he has to have a secretary, but he can't keep one. They won't put up with his rages. He can be terrifying when he's angry.' Stephen looked pleadingly at her. 'Of course, you may not feel you can even contemplate the idea, but . . . do you think you could meet him, just to see if you could face working for him?'

CHAPTER FOUR

'It could be another tricky move by Big Brother,' Annette warned Claudia half an hour later.

'I know, but somehow I believed Stephen. He has honest eyes, and he's the worrying type; I'm sure he wouldn't be able to lie very well. If you had heard him, you would have believed him, Annette—there's no doubt that he's very worried about his father. He's very fond of him, but a little frightened of him, too. He said his father was very like Ellis: obstinate and hot-tempered, very difficult to deal with, especially when he was ill or upset—and ... Oh, I could just imagine the old man, and I felt very sorry for him.'

'Hmm,' said Annette, frowning. 'Sure this Stephen wasn't just playing on your feelings?'

'I don't think so. Anyway, where's the harm in agreeing to meet the old man? He may hate me, he may throw me out before I've even shaken hands with him. Apparently, he's quite unpredictable at the moment. He needs help, but he hates anyone knowing he needs it. He's proud and touchy, and if someone shows any sort of pity for him he sacks them on the spot. Stephen says he is at his wit's end to know what to do for his father.'

'Why is it Stephen dealing with this? Didn't you say he was the younger brother? Why isn't Ellis getting his father a secretary?'

'Well, that's it,' said Claudia drily. 'Apparently, Ellis is one of the people his father has quarrelled with—he told Ellis to get out of his house and stay out, or he would set his dogs on him. There are three of them, Stephen says, Alsatians that sound more like wolves—they would tear someone limb from limb if the old man gave the order, and Ellis hasn't dared go back since.'

Annette grimaced. 'I don't like the sound of the dogs much, do you? I mean, they might tear you limb from limb if the old man told them to!'

Claudia pulled a wry face. 'Well, I'm not crazy about the thought of them, no. I'll see how I feel when I go there tomorrow with Stephen. If I'm not back by the time you start serving dinner, call the police!'

'That isn't funny!' Annette said grimly. 'Remember last time you had an appointment with a Lefèvre! You got yourself locked in that suite all night—and I'm still not sure you've told us the whole truth about what happened in there!'

Claudia went pink and scowled. 'Look, I tell you what—when Stephen comes, you can meet him and see what you think of him!'

Stephen arrived next day promptly at eleven-thirty, having asked her to have lunch with him on the way to meet his father. He shyly shook hands with Annette and Pierre and made a polite remark about having very much enjoyed the meal he had eaten in the restaurant the other night.

Pierre took on that air of ineffable satisfaction which a good French cook feels about his food. 'Ah, yes? Thank you.' He waited happily for further compliments, but his wife changed the subject.

'Do you work for your brother's corporation?' she asked, and, turning to smile at her, Stephen nodded.

'In a way. I have been working over here in the UK for a year now, though, on some research work, at Cambridge. I have been given two years off by the corporation, to allow me to do this research, and after that I'll be going back to work in Switzerland.'

'You and your brother speak perfect English,' said Annette. 'Are you Swiss or...?'

Claudia was embarrassed by all these searching questions. What on earth must Stephen think of them, being so curious? If he resented the questions, however, he didn't show it. He just nodded, still smiling.

'We are Swiss, yes! We were both born there. Our mother was born in Scotland, though—and our father spent several years at Cambridge, doing postgraduate work, after taking his degree in Geneva. He was a scientist, too. Our parents wanted us to specialise in languages so we had special tutors as soon as we could read and write. The corporation is multinational, and we need to be able to talk to our various national companies.'

'Now that we will soon have a united Europe, we all need to talk to each other,' said Pierre. 'But, of course, in Switzerland, you speak French, German and Italian, anyway, so you have an advantage over the rest of us.'

Stephen laughed. 'It helps, I suppose!'

'Now, the English have never been good at languages!' Pierre said, turning his attention to the old enemy, one eye mischievously on his wife. 'Too lazy. They have always expected other people to learn English.'

'Not any more! We're learning languages fast now,' said Annette, bristling. 'If we're talking about people being chauvinistic, what about the French? They invented the word...'

'Let's go before the war starts,' Claudia said to Stephen, and they left the husband and wife still locked in Anglo-French discussions and slipped away.

The roads out of London were as crowded as usual, and it took them quite some time to get through the outer suburbs, but eventually they pulled up outside an old hotel, set among green lawns, beside the upper reaches of the Thames.

'I've booked in here for lunch,' Stephen said, looking at Claudia uncertainly. 'They do a very good meal here. I hope you like it.'

'It's enchanting,' she said, staring at the gleam of water she could see through bare, wintry branches at the end of the hotel gardens. 'I don't really know this side of London, at all. It's very odd, the way Londoners seem to stay in their own part of the city and rarely venture out into other districts. They always say that London isn't so much a city as a series of villages, you know.'

They lunched beside a window looking down over the river. The food was as good as Stephen had promised; nothing spectacular, just excellent English cooking—a home-made vegetable soup, perfect roast beef and crisp vegetables, with which they drank a glass of red wine each, with a delicate orange mousse to finish with, and then some really delicious coffee.

While they ate they talked, mainly about old Mr Lefèvre, although the way Stephen talked about his father told her as much about Stephen himself as about the old man. His eyes were amused and wry as he tried in advance to apologise for his father's crotchety manner.

'He can't come to terms with losing his sight. He tries to pretend it hasn't happened, and when the truth is forced on him he gets very angry, very frustrated.'

'That's understandable,' Claudia said sympathetically.

'Oh, yes, but you're going to need a lot of patience.' He shot her an anxious look. 'But if you can only forgive him for those little flare-ups, and get to know him, I'm sure you'll like him.' He broke off, grimacing. 'I'm pushing you, and I didn't want to do that. I will understand if you feel you can't take him on, honestly. I don't want to force you into doing something you really don't want to do.'

Claudia smiled at him. 'I promise you, I'll only agree to take the job if I think I can handle it.'

She could already see one reason why she shouldn't take the job—the difficulty of travelling to and from the centre of London each day. It would be exhausting, very expensive, and make it difficult to attend auditions, see her voice coach or go to the gym.

On the other hand, she thought later, at the house, this would be a lovely place to work. Quentin Lefèvre lived in a comfortable Edwardian house with art nouveau stained glass windows, high ceilings, solid mahogany doors and furniture which exactly matched the architecture. Behind the house, gardens stretched down to the river; green lawns, wintry flower beds, and the silvery gleam of water through bare branches.

A slight, elegant Frenchwoman wearing a very chic little black dress, opened the door to them and smiled a wry welcome to Stephen. 'He has been waiting for you on the edge of his chair for most of the morning! He is not happy.'

'Oh, dear,' said Stephen, leaning forward to kiss the woman on both cheeks, French style.

'You may well say, "Oh, dear!"' she said drily. She had fine, dark hair liberally sprinkled now with silver, her make-up was perfection and she carried herself with poise and assurance. She made Claudia feel clumsy and over-colourful as Stephen introduced them.

'This is Claudia, I told you about her. Claudia, this is Celeste—she makes sure this house runs smoothly, I hate to think what would happen without her.'

Claudia offered her hand and Celeste took it, studying her thoughtfully. 'Hmm . . .' she murmured, and Claudia hoped that did not signify disapproval.

'You had better hurry,' was all she said, though. 'He is getting nasty!'

Claudia was getting very nervous about meeting Quentin Lefèvre, and as soon as she set eyes on him she could see she had had good cause to be worried. One look, and she knew just what Ellis Lefèvre would look like when he was seventy: hair white, face lined and bony, fierce with pride, his body long and thin and stooping. Quentin Lefèvre looked like a blind old eagle, perched in a high and lonely place, screaming his rage at the empty skies.

'So, you want a job?' he snapped at Claudia, after Stephen had introduced her, and for a second she almost snapped back, Not with you! But then she took a second look at the old man and she couldn't walk out on him. He might be difficult and prickly, but he was very unhappy, and he needed help.

'Yes, sir,' she said politely.

He asked her about her secretarial qualifications, and she was honest in reply. 'I'm not the best in the world, but I am adequate.'

He laughed brusquely. 'Adequate, hah?' He had a very strong accent, not one she recognised, and nothing like that of either of his sons. 'Well, I will dictate. You have a pad, a pencil?'

He dictated rapidly and she managed to get it all down, then she put the letter into the computer and printed it out, read it back to him while he listened intently, those blind eyes staring straight ahead.

'Hmm, yes. Adequate,' he said without enthusiasm. 'I like to work very early in the morning,' he said. 'I don't sleep much, so I get up at six every day, take a walk in the garden, have breakfast and I am ready to start work by seven.'

'Seven?' she repeated in horror. 'I'm sorry, I don't think I could get here by seven—it will take me an hour at the very least to make the journey.'

'Hmm...' he said again, his silvery brows lifting, then he said, 'Look out of the window.'

'Out of the...?'

'Window, girl, window,' he snarled.

Baffled, and wondering if he was a little crazy, Claudia went to the window and looked out.

'See the building at the far end of the gardens, by the river?' Quentin asked.

'The sort of cottage?' she asked, staring at the black-and-white mock Tudor building she could just see through the trees.

'It's a boathouse. Not that I ever go on the river, but the previous owners did. There are still a couple of boats in the lower part, but the floor above is a small flat, just a bedroom, a sitting-room, a kitchen and bathroom. Stephen can take you down there and show you. It isn't big, but it is comfortable, so I'm told. Haven't been in there, myself. It would save you the trouble and expense of travelling to London and back every day.'

Claudia was taken aback and didn't know what to say for a moment, then she nervously said, 'I suppose

it would, but you see there's my career to think
of——'

'Your career?' barked Quentin Lefèvre, scowling.
'What are you talking about?'

'I'm an actress,' she began and he interrupted
impatiently.

'An actress, Goddammit? An actress? What do I
want with an actress? I need a secretary. Stephen?
Where's Stephen? Why did my son bring you here to
meet me, if you don't want to work for me?'

'I do, sir,' she hurriedly assured him. 'At the
moment, I'm not working in the theatre. I'm between
parts, I'm resting, as we say...'

Quentin's heavy brows met above those sightless
eyes. 'And how long is it since you had a job?'

She flushed. 'Well... Not recently... I haven't had
much luck lately——'

'Aren't you any good at it?' Quentin brutally asked
and she flinched, resenting the question, even though
it was one she had been asking herself for a long, long
time now. But you couldn't let yourself think like that.
Confidence was everything in the theatre. You had to
believe you were good, you would make it, you just
needed the lucky break, the big chance. If you once
started doubting yourself you were finished.

'Yes, I am,' she said defiantly, her colour high, and
Quentin put his head to one side, listening to her
angry, shaking voice, but what he was thinking she
could not tell from his face. 'Anyway,' she said after
a pause, 'if I'm to live here, I shall need to have time
off if my agent gets me an audition. Or for my various
lessons—I have voice training once a week and I need
to do my physical training; dancing and fencing and
gym... You have to be fit, of course.'

'Hmm...' Quentin muttered. 'And exactly how much time off does this add up to during the week?'

'That isn't easy to say. For certain, it will mean one afternoon off for voice and physical training—and, if there are auditions, maybe another day? But not more than that a week. Parts don't come up every week.'

Quentin tapped his fingers on the desk grimly for a moment, then said brusquely, 'Oh, very well. But you cannot go to more than one audition a week, and I'd like you to fit your voice training et cetera into the weekend, if you can.'

'I'll try,' she promised, in relief.

'Good.' Quentin picked up the telephone from his desk, barked, 'Stephen! Come here.'

Stephen hurried into the room and his father curtly told him to take Claudia to see the boathouse. Stephen showed no surprise, merely nodded, and Claudia realised that he and his father must have discussed the idea of letting her use the boathouse flat.

As they made their way down the paved path which ran between the smooth green lawns, Stephen looked sideways at her and asked eagerly, 'What did you think of him?' She hesitated and he grimaced. 'You can be honest! I know he isn't easy to get on with!'

'No, he isn't,' she frankly admitted then. 'But somehow, I rather liked him, even though he did remind me of your brother.'

Stephen laughed. 'I told you that, too. That's why they quarrel so violently. I'm trying to persuade my father to forgive Ellis, but even if I did I don't know that Ellis would forgive him. They're two of a kind.'

Stephen waved her into the boathouse and followed her up a flight of stairs, to the upper floor.

The flat comprised a small bathroom, a fully fitted kitchen, a bedroom with pale green walls, dark green curtains and carpet, and a spacious, light-filled sitting-room with white walls, a blue carpet, blue curtains and simple white leather couch and chairs. The effect of the rooms in wintry sunlight was oddly Mediterranean; she found it hard to believe that when she looked out of the high, wide windows she would see a grey English sky, bare trees along the grey waters of the river, birds shivering in the chilly wind.

'What do you think?' asked Stephen, watching her delighted expression.

'It's lovely! I only have one room in my sister's flat, so this seems like a lot of space to me!'

He grinned happily. 'So you will take the job?' he pressed, and perhaps there was something of his brother in him after all. He certainly went for what he wanted, in his own way. She looked uncertainly at him and Stephen frowned. 'What's wrong? It isn't Ellis? I told you, he never visits my father, and, anyway, he's going to Japan for a month this evening. You needn't worry about having any trouble with him.'

'I wasn't,' Claudia lied, relaxing now that she knew Ellis would be far away. A month was a long time. 'When would you want me to start?'

'How about at once?' said Stephen, grinning, and when they rejoined Quentin Lefèvre he, also, asked her to start immediately.

'I am writing my autobiography and I want to get on with it!' he said, offering a salary that was more than she had expected.

Stephen drove her back to Mayfair. It was dark by the time he pulled up outside the back entrance of the restaurant, under a street lamp.

'I am very glad I thought of asking you to work for my father!' he said, smiling at her. 'He liked you, I could tell. I so want him to be happy, Claudia. Writing his life story will be a kind of therapy for him, I think. It could help him come to terms with his blindness.'

'I'll do my best to help him,' she promised, and Stephen's eyes glowed with gratitude.

'Thank you.' He leaned forward and kissed her lightly on the cheek, to her surprise, but it was a brotherly kiss, nothing to worry her, and when he drew back she smiled at him.

'I'll see you tomorrow, then, Stephen.' She got out of the car and watched him drive away, then turned to go into the restaurant, but stopped dead, her heart in her mouth, as someone moved out of the dark shadows around the building.

She was just getting ready to scream for help when the man came out into the yellow circle of the street light, and she recognised the powerful face, the black hair, the cold grey eyes.

'Oh, it's you!' she breathed with relief, and then suspicion shot through her. What was he doing here? Had he known she was going down to see his father, and when she would be arriving back? Had Stephen lied to her, after all? Was Ellis behind the scheme to get her to work for their father? But she didn't have a chance to ask him any of those questions.

'What the hell were you doing with my brother?' Ellis bit out with a black frown, walking towards her, making her very aware just how tall he was, and how disturbing.

'Why? Does he have to have your permission to date girls?' Claudia asked with furious mockery, and saw his eyes flash.

'Oh, it was a date, was it?' His voice was harsh, thick with rage, and she was convinced by it. No, Ellis had not known she was out with Stephen. His eyes were very hard and narrow as he stared down at her. 'So I did see him kiss you! I thought I'd imagined it. How long has this been going on? I wasn't even aware he had ever met you!'

'It's none of your business!' she said, side-stepping him and making a dash for the back door of the restaurant.

He was faster than her; he caught her before she reached the door, his hand clamping down on her shoulder and spinning her round.

'No, you don't! I want to know how you met him, what exactly is going on between the pair of you!'

'Don't you bully me! I'm not telling you anything!' She struggled against his grip and he forced her against the wall and stood in front of her, barring any attempt at escape.

'Oh, I think you'll tell me what I want to know,' he said, his voice silky with menace. 'Because we'll stay here until you do.'

She gave him a contemptuous stare. 'Oh, well, if you're going to inflict yourself on me, I suppose I'll have to tell you. Anything to get away from you!'

Her tone was a verbal slap in the face, and Ellis took it as one, his face tightening, his grey eyes glittering. He didn't say anything, but somehow she got the impression that that was because she had temporarily deprived him of the power of speech. Perhaps no woman had ever said such a thing to him before? Well, if so, perhaps it was time it happened! He was due for a lesson. She met his furious stare head on, refusing to be frightened of him.

'Stephen came to the restaurant again yesterday, we got into conversation, and he asked me out today. We had lunch by the river, and then drove back here.' She made it sound very casual, and she carefully left out any mention of his father or the job she had just accepted, ending with a cool lift of one eyebrow as she asked him, 'Satisfied?'

'Was Stephen?' asked Ellis, with a sneer, which sent a wave of hot blood up her face.

'You've got a disgusting mind!'

'I'm a man myself,' he said with an unsmiling shrug. 'I know what a woman like you does to the imagination.'

'A woman like me?' she repeated, insult in every line of her. 'What do you mean—a woman like me?'

'You're temptation with a capital T,' he said drily. 'It didn't occur to me that it was a mistake to bring Stephen here and let him catch sight of you. I've never had any trouble with Stephen that way in the past. He's never trespassed on my territory before.'

She took a rough, shaky breath. 'Your territory? Your territory? I hope you're not referring to me! Because, if you are, then let me tell you I am nothing of the kind!'

Ellis took no notice of her; he seemed to be talking to himself, his voice cool. 'But then perhaps he didn't realise that that was what he was doing. Stephen can be quite dim at times.'

'I don't think Stephen is at all dim,' she said icily. 'In fact, it's hard to believe Stephen is your brother. He's so easy to talk to, kind and thoughtful, a good companion—totally unlike you in almost every way...'

His mouth twisted. 'The description doesn't sound like me, I agree! But it doesn't sound wildly exciting, either. And you chose to date him? Either I have been underestimating my brother—or...?' He lifted his brows at her, his grey eyes gleaming with mockery. 'Or you went out with him to get back at me! Do I detect a malicious glint in those lovely green eyes? Is that what you did? Were you playing games, Claudia?'

'No, I was not!' she muttered, tensing as he let his gaze deliberately wander down over her, a sensuous curve to his smile. 'Look, I answered your question, I told you what you wanted to know. Now, will you let me go?'

'Oh, not yet!' he said, staring at her mouth.

Her pulses began to thud crazily, and she made another dive to escape, only to be trapped again, this time more dangerously, with Ellis leaning both hands on the wall on either side of her, and his long, lean body forced down on top of hers. His head came down and with a wild gasp of panic she tried to escape the searching mouth, but he lifted a hand from the wall and clasped her throat, his thumb pressing up under her chin to lift her head.

The pressure didn't so much hurt as threaten pain if she resisted, and made her helpless to stop him kissing her, his mouth hot and insistent against her lips, forcing them apart and passionately exploring her mouth. His other hand moved, too, sliding down her body in a lingering caress, making heat flow through her flesh with every brush of his fingers.

When he slowly lifted his head, she had her eyes closed and she was trembling violently. She had to take a deep breath before she could open her eyes and look at him without betraying what he had aroused in her, the unexpected force of the desire, the need, the ache of pleasure.

'Why can't men ever keep their hands to themselves?' she hoarsely muttered. 'What on earth makes you think every woman you meet is going to fall into your arms the minute you click your fingers? I suppose it's because you're so rich? Your money usually impresses the hell out of most women. Well, it doesn't mean a thing to me. Money doesn't impress me, nor does the caveman stuff you just tried out. I prefer a man I can respect and like, and you don't qualify on either count!'

She stopped only because she had run out of breath, but Ellis didn't yell back at her, as she expected. He was staring down at her, his eyes wells of dark violence, his face drawn tight, but a little tic jumping beside his mouth.

That look scared her. Somehow, it seemed, she had hit Ellis Lefèvre where it hurt, and he was very, very angry. Before she could work out exactly what she had said to make him look like that, he let his hands drop to his sides, swung on his heel and strode across the pavement to where a sleek Porsche was parked. Claudia watched him get behind the wheel, heard the door slam, the engine fire, and a second later the car streaked away into the night.

CHAPTER FIVE

CLAUDIA couldn't move for several minutes, she was feeling so shaken. She had managed to send Ellis Lefèvre away before he realised quite how violently he attracted her, but she did not feel at all relieved, she felt cold and miserable. She couldn't understand it. She didn't like the man; he was arrogant, selfish, domineering, how could anybody like him? Why should she be depressed because she had told him the blunt truth about himself? He thought his money gave him *carte blanche* to do as he liked, he thought his money could buy him anything—even a woman.

Well, not this woman! she thought, her face burning and her eyes stinging with unshed tears. She got out a handkerchief and blew her nose defiantly, then banged her way through the door, almost walking right into her sister.

'Look out!' Annette yelled, clutching the large glass bowl of trifle which she was carrying. 'Oh! I thought I was going to drop it for a minute. How many times have I told you not to go barging about like that, Claudia?' She put the bowl of trifle on to the dessert trolley.

Claudia sat down on a chair, chill perspiration dewing her forehead. She kept remembering that look Ellis had given her. Each time her blood ran cold.

Annette eagerly asked, 'Well, how did the interview go? What was the old man like? Did you get the job?'

Claudia wanted to scream at her—Leave me alone! But she couldn't, so she just stared blankly, and Annette stared back, beginning to look worried.

'Claudia, what ever's wrong? Aren't you feeling OK? Has something happened?'

Looking round from his inspection of the pans on the stove, Pierre said with wry amusement, 'Let the poor girl answer one question at a time, *chérie*! Rat tat tat, like a machine gun, you go. Give her time!'

'Oh, you get on with your cooking. She's my sister, not yours. Claudia! What's the matter with you, for heaven's sake?'

'Nothing's the matter,' Claudia managed huskily. 'I'm tired, that's all.' She took a deep breath and went on rather more calmly, 'It's been a long day, but the interview went well, I think I can manage Mr Lefèvre, and . . .' she even forced a sort of smile ' . . . I got the job.'

'Wonderful!' her sister said, beaming, and quite unaware, thank heavens, that Claudia was less than rapturously happy. 'Well, tell us . . . What's the salary?'

'Excellent.' Claudia rattled off the details and Annette looked even more cheerful.

'Well, that's great! And it should be quite interesting, typing a book for someone . . . If it's his life story, it might be full of fascinating gossip.'

'Not about anyone I would know,' Claudia said drily.

'Oh, Claudia . . . Before I forget,' Pierre suddenly said. 'You had a phone call half an hour ago. From some boyfriend . . . He wouldn't leave his name.'

Claudia looked sharply at him. 'Did you tell him where I was?'

'No, but I said you should be back any minute, so maybe he'll ring again. He wouldn't leave his name or number.' Pierre winked. 'He wanted to be a mystery man!'

Annette raised her brows curiously at her sister. 'Who is this? A new guy? Why all the secrecy?' Her face changed. 'He isn't married, is he, Claudia? You haven't got mixed up with a married man?'

'No, nothing like that,' Claudia said, knowing very well who had rung, and reluctant to tell them. 'He's nobody important... Just... someone I met at the hotel, who has been chasing me, OK?' They were staring, and she rushed on hurriedly before they could ask any more questions. 'But I was telling you about Mr Lefèvre. He is rather formidable, but I had been warned, so I was forearmed, and I think I may be able to manage him. I might even get to like him. Stranger things have happened.' She gave her sister a hesitant look. 'One thing, though—I will have to stay there until this book is finished.'

Annette stiffened. 'What?'

Claudia was faintly flushed and defiant as she answered. 'Well, the old man wakes up very early and likes to begin work at seven, and there's no way I could get there by that time unless I got up in the middle of the night, but there is a self-contained flat——'

'Claudia, I warned you!' Annette burst out, frowning heavily. 'This is what happened before, with the son, with what's-his-name... Elliot?'

'Ellis,' Claudia muttered. How could Annette forget his name?

'OK, Ellis,' Annette said impatiently. 'What difference does it make? Remember how he asked you to work for him and then made you stay in his suite all night—and it is happening all over again, but this time with his father——'

'His father?' Pierre interrupted, laughing. 'How old is he?'

'Oh, keep out of this!' Annette said, but Claudia answered him, her green eyes amused.

'Sixty-five...maybe seventy? Well, that's my guess.' Claudia made a laughing face, and Pierre roared with amusement.

'But that's nothing! A spring chicken! Did he chase you around the desk? Pinch your pretty behind?'

'Neither,' she said, looking at her sister. 'Oh, come on, Annette! The man is far too old. He is not the remotest threat to any woman. If you saw him! He is worn and tired, has grey hair, his face is like a cracked old map...and he's blind into the bargain!'

'Maybe you're right,' Annette said sulkily. 'But he has two sons, and I don't like the sound of this flat business. What it really means is that you will be living in that house with them!'

'No, not in the house. The flat is over a boathouse, and it has its own front door.'

'Doors can be unlocked!'

'But not if they're bolted from the inside, and I checked—there's a bolt at the top and bottom of the front door. I am going to be very safe in there, Annette. And, anyway, Ellis Lefèvre is leaving for Japan tonight. And the other brother, Stephen, is a pussycat—you've met him, you know he's a darling, and no problem. So stop fussing.'

Annette threw up her hands. 'All right. All right. I won't say another word.'

'Not even "I told you so", if anything does happen?' taunted Pierre, but she gave him a threatening glance.

'You be careful, or I'll take the rest of the day off and you'll be left alone to serve the customers and cook the meal.'

Pierre put a hand over his mouth and turned back to his stove, but his shoulders were shaking with laughter.

Claudia pretended to laugh, but she did not sleep very well that night. She was too disturbed by those moments in Ellis Lefèvre's arms. She kept tossing and turning in bed, too restless to relax, her body aching with aroused sensuality. What had he been doing, waiting for her out there? Why had he come to see her again? Had he meant to try to talk her into taking that job with him?

She had expected that he wouldn't come near her again, after she had poured that soup over his head. She gave a slightly hysterical giggle, remembering the way he had glared, with cucumber in his hair and cress on his cheek. He had stalked out looking as if he wanted to kill her, but he had come back, and that made her heart flip like a landed fish. He had been furious, but he had still come to find her again.

Well, OK, she argued with herself—he's persistent, but then you know that. Nobody runs a huge, worldwide business like his without the ability to keep coming back in spite of setbacks. Ellis Lefèvre was a determined, tenacious man, who kept after what he wanted, and, for some reason, at the moment he seemed to want her.

A hot flush burned her cheeks and she closed her eyes, biting down on her lower lip. The very thought made her feel weak, and that was so stupid! It was no compliment that a man like Ellis Lefèvre should feel a passing fancy for her. He wasn't in love with her. It was something more basic he had on his mind.

He wanted to get her into bed, and then he would forget all about her.

Was that all he thought there was to it? A bargain, a deal, with the woman an object to be bought, acquired, made use of...a new toy for him to enjoy until it bored him?

Because that was all she would mean to him if she ever let herself get involved with him—a toy, a plaything, to be discarded for something newer and more exciting one day.

She turned over again, beating the pillow with a clenched fist. He wasn't doing that to her. Never. He was never going to get an inch closer again; she was not going to let her stupid body betray her, after this, never again, not now she knew how vulnerable she was to him.

She was red-eyed and weary in the morning, but she felt calmer. She had made a clear-cut decision. She knew just how she felt and what she was going to do about it. It was some help to know that by now Ellis would probably be well on his way to Japan and by the time he came back, in another month, if she was firm with herself, she would be immune to him.

Stephen picked her and her luggage up that afternoon, and drove her out to his father's house, cheerfully inviting Annette and Pierre to come and visit her one day, whenever they had some time off. The invitation reassured them—as, no doubt, it was meant to. Stephen had picked up the silent undertones of her sister's mood, her worried expression.

'Ring us every day!' Annette urged, all the same, her eyes full of warnings and forebodings.

'Yes, OK,' Claudia promised, her own eyes wry. How old did Annette think she was? Anyone would think she was setting out on a trip to the Amazon jungle instead of driving thirty miles out of London to stay with a very old man in a peaceful house by the river.

'Your sister is anxious about you?' Stephen guessed as they drove away, and she laughed, nodding.

'She thinks you might be a white slaver.'

He grinned. 'What a wonderful idea. Why didn't it occur to me?' Then he sobered. 'They must come and visit you, it will show them that they have no need to worry.'

'Annette always worries,' she assured him.

'She is much older than you?'

'Not so very much, but she grew up first, and still feels I'm just a kid. Didn't you have the same problem with your brother?'

Stephen grimaced. 'Oh, yes! Ellis has always thought that he knew how I should run my life! But then he thinks he should run everything. It is usually too tiring, trying to argue with him; it is easier to agree.'

She pretended to laugh, then very casually, she asked: 'Did you say he had gone to Japan?'

Stephen nodded. 'I expect he's there by now. I haven't heard otherwise, but then Ellis and I aren't what you might call close. We don't talk to each other every day. We haven't quarrelled, the way he and my father have—but we don't have that much in common. He's a businessman, and I'm a scientist—and there's quite a gulf between the two.'

'I suppose there must be,' she said vaguely, without real interest, staring out at the crowded London streets through which they drove. She would miss the city. Or would she? A few weeks in the countryside would be very peaceful, and might help her to forget she had ever met Ellis.

The little flat looked as immaculate as it had before, but today there were vases of russet and white chrysanthemums everywhere, giving the rooms even more colour and a lovely, smoky fragrance.

'How lovely!' Claudia admired, bending her face to breathe in the scent.

'Celeste thought some flowers would make you feel more at home,' Stephen said. 'She's tough, but very kind-hearted, by the way; try to make friends with her. She's important to my father, she has worked for him for years. She is French, but her husband was Swiss, a wonderful chef—he worked for my father, too, until he died fifteen years ago. Celeste has worn mourning ever since.'

'So she moved here with your father from Switzerland? You lived there, too? Don't you miss it?' Claudia asked as he set her cases down.

'Now and then,' he admitted. 'Not so much the city as the mountains—I love winters there, the whiteness of the snow, the blue skies, the sting of cold air on the face. I feel more alive there than I ever do anywhere else.'

'Did you come to England to be near your father?'

Stephen laughed. 'No, it was the other way round. I came to do this research at Cambridge, and my father came to be near me. Also, there are some excellent eye specialists in Britain, and he hoped one of them might be able to work miracles.' He gave her a wry smile, but there was pain in his eyes. 'Of course, none of them could.'

'I'm sorry,' she said gently, liking him more than ever.

Stephen shrugged. 'There's nothing we can do but try to help him get used to the truth. I hope you will be able to help him, Claudia. You have such a sympathetic personality...'

She wondered if Ellis would agree, but didn't say so, merely smiled back at Stephen, and said she would do what she could.

'I know you will.' He tried to shake off the bleak mood, looking around the sitting-room with a determined smile. 'And I hope you'll soon feel at home here.'

'I'm sure I shall,' she said. 'As soon as I've arranged a few of my own things around the place.' She opened the smaller of her cases, and began to unpack and set out some of her favourite possessions—family photographs in silver frames, which she had inherited from her grandfather, a travelling alarm clock, some books, some audio tapes. Stephen watched her with interest, occasionally picking something up and admiring it, studying the photos closely.

'You and your sister don't look alike, do you?' he said, and she laughed.

'No, any more than you look like your brother!'

He grimaced, nodding. 'I take after our mother. She died when I was in my teens.'

'Oh, I'm sorry,' Claudia said, and he smiled at her.

'It was a long time ago, now. I still miss her occasionally, but I'm used to not having her here now. I think Ellis misses her more—they were very close, although I actually looked more like her. It was Ellis who was her favourite, I knew that. That is odd, isn't it? Ellis resembles our father, yet the two of them fight like cat and dog.'

'Have they always quarrelled a great deal?'

'Always, but it has been worse since my father's sight went and he had to give up control of the business. He didn't want to do it, of course, and he

resents Ellis because of it—he's jealous, I suppose.
He still tries to keep in close touch with what is going
on, but it is difficult to run a multinational corporation when you are ill. There is too much pressure,
too many people trying to lobby you or even snatch
control away from you.'

Claudia made a disgusted face. 'How appalling! I
would have thought he would be glad to get away from
that sort of hassle.'

Stephen's mouth was crooked, and he laughed
shortly. 'When you have been used to holding the reins
of power, it isn't easy to let go of them. It had to
happen, it made sense to let Ellis take over, but Father
didn't like having to do it.'

'It wasn't Ellis's fault, though!' Claudia said in-
voluntarily, then bit her lip, wondering why on earth
it should matter to her. She didn't like him, so why
should it upset her to know that his father resented
him, was hostile to him? She hoped Stephen hadn't
noticed, and gave him a secret, sideways glance, but
he was frowning at the floor; he was quite unaware
of her, absorbed in his own thoughts.

'No, of course not,' he agreed. 'But when you're
ill and afraid, you stop being rational.'

She was to remember that next day, when she
greeted his father cheerfully, 'Good morning!' and
got a snarled reply.

'What's good about it?'

'Well, at least the sun is shining and the river is a
lovely bright silver!' she said, without thinking, and
got her head bitten off.

'As I can't see it, I'll have to take your word for
it. Now, will you eat your breakfast and let me eat
mine? And in future, Miss Thorburn, don't talk to
me while I'm eating! It gives me indigestion.'

She was flushed with horror at her own lack of tact and didn't dare say another word. As her sister always said, a hungry man was an angry man. She hoped he would be less touchy once he had eaten. He wasn't. If anything, he got worse as the day went on, and she had to keep biting her lip to stop herself snapping back at him. She kept reminding herself that he was a man under tremendous strain, she fought to stay calm and patient, but it was an uphill fight. Several times that first day, she almost handed in her notice and walked out, but she kept remembering Stephen's faith in her, and what he had said about his father being ill and afraid, and not very rational, and so she stayed. Perhaps once he got used to her he would be easier to deal with? Next day she faced him with trepidation, and he was just as morose and difficult as he had been the first day.

It was some consolation that what he was dictating to her was so fascinating. When he wasn't shouting or snapping at her, she could lose herself in the text she was keying into her word processor. Quentin Lefèvre seemed to have total recall, and his memories of his childhood in Switzerland were both sad and idyllic. He had lived in a shimmering white land-scape, gone to school on skis, skated over the frozen lakes and rivers near his home. It was a fairy-tale setting for a child—and yet at the heart of that childhood was a tragedy. His mother had died when he was six, and Claudia felt tears sting her eyes as she tapped out what the old man said about the effect that death had on him.

'Read that back to me,' he barked when she had finished, and she read, her voice husky and a little shaky.

'Have you got a cold?' he demanded, scowling. 'I don't want you near me if you aren't a hundred per cent fit!'

She swallowed, cleared her throat, and said she was fine, and they went on with the reading. Working for him was a permanent struggle for self-control. He was moody, surly, irritable; she learnt to recognise the signs of impending explosion, but it was never possible to avert it because Quentin's rage was not with her but with fate for having made him blind, and there was simply nothing to be done about that. Even her patience with him infuriated him.

'Don't humour me, girl!' he lashed out one day, towards the end of an exhausting afternoon. 'Stop agreeing with everything I say!'

'What do you want me to do? Be as disagreeable as you are?' Claudia snapped, then drew a shaky breath and turned pale, horrified.

'At least that wouldn't leave me feeling I was being treated like a child or an idiot!'

'I certainly didn't mean to make you feel like that!'

'Then why are you always so polite and careful what you say?' he muttered, turning his blind grey eyes in her direction, looking astonishingly like Ellis, his mouth turned down at the corners and his brows together. 'If it's raining and I say it's a sunny day, you'd damn well agree with me.'

'I'm sorry,' she said unhappily.

'Don't keep saying you're sorry, either! All the girls who come here are the same—silly, whimpering females, forever on the verge of tears! Stephen seemed to think you were different, but you're just like all the rest.'

'Well, if you bullied them the way you've bullied me, that isn't so surprising! You probably scared them out of their wits.' Claudia saw that there was no point in being polite and patient, any more. She might as well tell him what she really thought.

'They didn't have any wits to be scared out of!' he insisted, grimacing, then sat in silence for a moment, before asking roughly, 'Do I scare you?'

'Frequently,' she said, and there was a faint, tentative smile in her voice. Quentin Lefèvre turned his head, as if listening to something other than her words, then smiled rather drily.

'Maybe I am sometimes bad-tempered. If so, I am sorry. There! I've apologised. Now, will you stop acting like my nurse? Do you imagine I want a secretary with no brain? A robot to answer the telephone and type? What use is that to me? I want someone I can talk to, someone with brains.' His voice was rough. 'You are the only person so far who has read what I'm writing... So, tell me what you think!'

'I'm fascinated,' she said frankly. 'You've made me laugh and you've made me cry... I think it's wonderful stuff and it will be a big hit.'

His face slowly flushed. 'Thank you.'

From that moment on, his temper was less hair-trigger, his moods less black. Sometimes, he reverted, and she learnt when to tread warily, but at least they had begun to talk openly to each other.

'Stephen warned you not to argue with me?' he said one day, grimacing. 'Well, I'm not surprised. He never does, nor does Celeste, or my doctor. They soothe me and placate me and agree with everything I say, however crazy. Nobody really talks to me any more. I never hear what's happening in the corporation, nobody comes to see me; they report to Ellis now, they ignore me. I'm nobody, I've been marooned on a desert island.' He was getting excited again, his face wearing a dark flush, lines of temper around his mouth. 'Ellis has given orders that I shouldn't be told a damn thing! He makes sure he never comes near me, either.'

'Do you want to see him?' she asked, watching his face with attention.

Quentin stared into that interior darkness of his, frowning. 'I am his father. He should want to see me,' was all he said, fiercely.

She helped Celeste lay the table for dinner that evening, and tentatively asked her if she thought Quentin secretly missed his elder son, and Celeste gave her a wry look.

'Oh, yes! But he would die rather than admit it, and Ellis...he would die rather than risk being turned away at the front door. They are both like the Chinese—losing face is too important to them.' Standing back, she eyed the completed table, nodding in satisfaction. 'That will do! Thank you, *chérie*. You are going to make someone a useful wife, one day.'

Claudia laughed, but was secretly flattered. She liked Celeste; the cool, dry personality of the Frenchwoman was a mask for a far warmer and more affectionate nature. Celeste, like Quentin himself, was not easy to get to know.

When Stephen drove down the next time, Claudia raised the subject of Ellis with him, too. He only ever stayed for a few hours, usually for lunch, but it was pleasant to have his company and Claudia was becoming quite fond of him. He had a gentle, appealing personality which was strangely unlike that of either his father or his brother.

'He complained that Ellis had not been to see him, but when I asked if he wanted to see Ellis he just said

Ellis ought to want to see him.' She gave Stephen a laughing grimace, and he smiled back.

'That sounds like him! He can be as stubborn as a mule. Well, when Ellis comes home, I'll drop him a hint—but I don't know if he will take it. He's as bloody-minded and difficult as the old man.'

'And that's saying something,' Claudia grimaced, getting a quick, searching look from Stephen.

'How are you getting on with him now? I know he has been quite tough with you...'

'Well, I hope we're getting on rather better now. We had a bit of a row yesterday, a few very nasty moments, but ever since he has been quite good-tempered.' She paused, then grinned. 'For him!'

'You like him!' Stephen said, amused, and she nodded.

'I'm beginning to, now that I'm getting to know him.'

She was to go home for the weekend, her first weekend off, and Stephen offered to drive her back to London after lunch.

'So I'm going to have some peace and quiet, am I?' grunted Quentin Lefèvre, his lower lip stuck out mulishly.

'Will you miss me?' Claudia teased and got a startled look from Stephen, amazed to hear his father being teased, but Quentin gave a grunt of laughter.

'Miss you? As much as I would miss a wasp buzzing in my hair!'

On the drive to London, Stephen said, 'I couldn't believe my ears! My father actually laughed when you teased him! You're doing a wonderful job, Claudia. He hasn't smiled like that for months! I can't tell you how grateful I am.'

He asked her to have dinner with him that evening, but she had already promised to help in the restaurant that evening, so she agreed to a date with him on the Sunday lunchtime.

'We'll have a long, leisurely meal, and then I'll drive you back to my father's house afterwards,' he promised.

Annette was full of eager, excited questions when Claudia arrived at the flat. They had talked on the phone, but now she listened with fascination to fuller descriptions of Quentin, Celeste, the house, the flat above the boathouse, even the three wolfish Alsatians.

'But if they are let loose at night, how do you get through the garden to your flat?' she asked, frowning.

'Quentin eats dinner very early, he goes to bed at about nine-thirty. If I eat with him, the dogs aren't let out until I'm safely in the boathouse.'

'Oh, yes?' Annette said belligerently. 'And what if there's an emergency and you need to get back to the house in a hurry? If you were taken ill, for instance, or there was a fire, or an accident?'

'If I ever need to come back to the house, I'll have to ring the garage flat, which is where the chauffeur lives, and tell him to lock the dogs up again. He's in charge of them, you see. He feeds them and handles them.'

'What's he like?'

'Quiet. I rarely see him. Mr Lefèvre doesn't go out much, so he doesn't need his chauffeur often. George keeps busy doing other things, though, he works hard all by himself—mows the lawns, looks after the security system itself—the gates are electrified and so is the wall around the garden. Nobody can get in, except from the river, through the boathouse—and if

they did get through that way the dogs would have
them.'

'It would make me very nervous living like that!'
Annette said, and Claudia shrugged.

'You do get used to it quite quickly.'

Pierre yelled for both of them to come and help lay
the tables, so the subject of the Lefèvre household
was dropped. It was a hectic weekend, and by the time
Stephen picked her up on Sunday lunchtime Claudia
was shattered and very glad to see him.

He took her to a houseboat on the Thames, which
had been turned into a small, unique, exclusive and
very expensive restaurant. There were only five tables,
but the food was incredible and Claudia had a wonderful time. It was dusk by the time Stephen returned
her to his father's house. She called in to reassure
Quentin that she was back, had a drink with him and
Stephen, and then walked down through the gardens
to her own place, deciding that she needed an early
night. She had eaten too much already, so she
showered, drank some warm milk, and then went to
bed, falling asleep almost at once.

She slept heavily for some hours, and then a sound
woke her and she sat up in bed, eyes wide and startled.
Someone else was in the flat. She could hear breathing,
movements, there was a crack of light under her
bedroom door.

How could anyone have got in? she thought,
dazedly, and then it came to her in a flash of horrified
recollection—she had been so tired last night that she
had forgotten to bolt her front door. The intruder
must have come from the river—nobody could get
past the Alsatians in the garden!

She put a shaky hand out to the phone to ring
George, in the garage, but as she did so her door

opened. She saw the shape of a tall man outlined against the light in the corridor, and gasped in shock.

'Who the hell is that?' the intruder grated, and Claudia had a second shock as she recognised that deep, horribly familiar voice. She didn't need to answer. The bedroom light was switched on and Ellis Lefèvre stared at her across the room, his black brows swooping upwards incredulously.

'You? What on earth are you doing here?' His eyes narrowed, hardened, glittering, and he turned an angry, dark red. The way he looked at her made Claudia feel sick, suddenly. She had known he was furious with her, but she could see then that he actually hated her. There was bitter distaste in his face. Before she could get out a syllable, he said harshly, 'Oh, I get it—stupid of me not to work it out at once! Stephen installed you here, did he? Does my father know? No, of course he doesn't, he wouldn't let Stephen keep a woman in this flat.' Those fierce eyes flicked down over her with contempt, from her ruffled, dishevelled hair and flushed face, her pale, bare shoulders, to the filmy white silk nightdress which clung to her breasts, revealing rather than hiding them.

Claudia's face burned, as much with rage as with embarrassment. 'No, you're mistaken,' she began, but Ellis's voice rose over hers, drowning her explanation.

'It's you and Stephen who've made the mistake. He isn't using my father's home as a love nest. You can get dressed and get out of here tonight.'

CHAPTER SIX

CLAUDIA was so violently angry that she was trembling. She couldn't speak because her head was choked with all the things she wanted to say to Ellis. She wanted to tell him precisely what she thought of him, and even more she wanted to hit the man. But he had her at a disadvantage. He was fully dressed, in formal dark clothes which somehow made what he had just said to her even more shocking—and she was in bed, in a transparent nightdress. It made her too self-conscious, it made her vulnerable, it even made the insults he had thrown at her seem justified, and she had to change that.

She had to get out of bed and get dressed—but she couldn't do that while he watched her. She wasn't even getting up and going into the bathroom to dress, until he had left this room. It made her feel quite ill to imagine those grey eyes of his flicking up and down her body as she got out of bed. She had to get him out of this room before she got up and dressed.

'Well? Nothing to say?' he sneered. 'Or are you trying to work out some way of persuading me to change my mind?' His eyes had a dangerous brilliance as they wandered down over her, and his smile made her face burn. 'Well, now, that would depend on what you were thinking of offering me. I might be tempted—with the right offer.'

'You... You...' Claudia couldn't get the words out, she was too distraught, and she had to calm down. She tensely counted to ten in her head, her dilated green eyes still holding his mocking stare. She willed herself to slow down—her heartbeat, her breathing, her mind itself. She had to be cool. If she was to manoeuvre him out of this room, she had to have herself under control. What had she learnt about him if not that he would meet anger with anger, force with force?

She took a long, long breath and managed to say quietly: 'Will you wait in the sitting-room, Mr Lefèvre? I will get dressed and join you.'

His mouth twisted with icy mockery. 'Or I could get undressed, and join you!'

He took a step closer to the bed and Claudia felt her pulse leap disturbingly.

She still struggled to stay calm, her voice level, 'You may think that's funny, Mr Lefèvre, but I'm afraid I'm not amused.'

'Neither am I,' he said, a faint huskiness in his voice suddenly, and he took another step. His eyes glittered; their black pupils dilated with sexual excitement as he stared at her smooth-skinned, bare shoulders and her half-naked breasts.

Claudia clutched the sheet and pulled it up to hide her body from that arrogant, intimate assessment. 'Get out of here!' she burst out, beginning to be really scared. 'Don't you come any closer or——'

'Or what?' he asked, suddenly right beside the bed, and she couldn't breathe at all, her mouth was dry and her ears were deafened by the sound of her own blood pumping far too rapidly around her body. 'What will you do if I come closer, Claudia?' he whispered, and she trembled, shrinking back against the pillow.

'Show me what you're going to do, Claudia,' he said in that low, husky, voice, his mouth curving in a taunt, and suddenly he was on the bed, sitting on the edge of it and reaching for her.

'No!' she cried out in panic, beating his hands away, but she was too late to stop him.

He pulled her up towards him with those strong, sinewy hands of his, his grip so fierce that he hurt her. She struggled wildly, her red-gold hair tossing around her, but she couldn't break free, and Ellis held her captive for a second, inches away from him, staring down into her wide, panic-stricken green eyes. She could hear the rough drag of his breathing, see a little tic going beside his mouth.

'I wanted you the minute I set eyes on you,' he muttered. 'Why did you turn me down and take my brother? Why, damn you?' He shook her, his fingers digging into her flesh, and she couldn't look away from his face, she was half-afraid, and yet half-excited, too. He wanted her. Her pulses were going crazy at the thought. She had known that, though, hadn't she? He wanted her—but how many others had he wanted, and briefly had, only to forget them? Was that what she wanted to happen to her? That wasn't the sort of relationship she wanted with any man. Lust burnt out like a struck match; love was the only fire that lasted.

She had to stop him while she still could, so she said sharply, 'I prefer Stephen, but that's my business, not yours. Just let go of me, will you?'

His face was dark with angry colour, and although he was listening to her he didn't let go. 'Prefer Stephen?' he grated. 'I don't believe you—you couldn't look at me the way you do if you were the type to prefer Stephen...'

What did he mean by that, she wondered, shaken? How did she look at him? She wished she knew, so that she could make sure she never did it again.

She pretended to laugh and said scornfully, 'You flatter yourself! Try to get this through your head, Mr Lefèvre... I'm simply not interested in you at all!'

His lip curled back in an animal snarl, and she couldn't help thinking of the dogs prowling the grounds outside. She shivered; Ellis was as unpredictable and as potentially deadly as one of the Alsatians. It would be folly to forget that.

Holding his stare she said carefully, in a cool voice, 'For the last time, Mr Lefèvre—I don't want you, and if you don't get out of my room immediately, I shall——'

She got no further. His head descended, his mouth clamped down over hers, and her words were stifled by the force of that angry kiss. She fought him, writhing and pulling back, but he would not let her go and at last she was too tired to fight any more. Her head had clouded, she was so weak that the room swam around her, making her so dizzy she had to shut her eyes. She went limp, half fainting in his grip, and Ellis's hands slipped from her arms and moved around her to draw her closer.

The violence drained out of his kiss; it softened into heated passion, coaxing her lips to part and permit his invasion, and Claudia shuddered into a reluctant, shamed response.

A moment later, Ellis pushed her backwards on to the bed, and she was too absorbed in kissing him back to resist. He came down with her, lying full length on the bed, murmuring huskily without words as his mouth moved against hers.

He pulled the narrow silk straps of her nightdress from her shoulders, and his fingertips gently stroked along her bare skin. Claudia's hands clenched in his thick, warm hair, a terrible excitement pulsing in her

body. She couldn't think of anything while he was
touching her like that; she felt as if she were trapped
in a dream, a hot, sensual dream.

Ellis caressed her long, pale throat with one hand,
while the other slid downwards, pushing her nightdress down with it, to bare her breasts. He cupped
one, his palm beneath the full weight of her warm
flesh, his fingers softly stroking upward, his thumb
rubbing her hard, round nipple.

She gave a low, deep moan, trembling violently. She
hadn't known that anything could give so much
pleasure. The wildness of her own response took her
by surprise and made her helpless to stop him or even
to want to resist. She would have to fight her own
desire as well as his if she tried to stop him, because
she wanted him fiercely. She put her arms around his
body and touched him with passion, twisting restlessly on the bed, making high, excited sounds in her
throat.

He slid his mouth from her lips to her throat, then
downwards, very slowly, an inch at a time, over the
warm, smooth skin of her breasts until he closed his
mouth around one of her nipples, startling a cry of
wild desire from her.

She held his head there, groaning, as his hands
moved even lower to her hips, her thighs. The heat
inside her was burning her up, she forgot everything
but her need for him.

That was when Ellis suddenly lifted his head, and
knelt up, staring down at her flushed face and half-
naked, visibly aroused body. Claudia took a few
seconds to realise that he had stopped making love to
her. She opened her eyes quite slowly and focused on
him in trembling bewilderment.

He was smiling, but it was not a pleasant smile. His eyes were chilly and his mouth had cruelty in the lines of it.

'Did Stephen get the same response, I wonder?' he drawled, and the ice of his voice made her turn white, and she began to shake. 'I doubt it. Well, I wanted to prove a point, and I proved it, didn't I? If I wanted you, I could have you, for all your protests.' He skimmed a glance over her from head to foot, then shrugged. 'But I don't think I'll bother.'

He got off the bed and ran a hand over his hair, smoothing it down, straightened his tie, flicked one of her long, red-gold hairs from his jacket shoulder.

'You can spend the rest of the night here, but tomorrow first thing I want you gone,' he said coolly, walking away.

Claudia was too numb with shock to move or speak. She stared as the door closed quietly behind him, and she was alone again, her eyes stinging with tears. If it didn't hurt so much, she would almost have believed she had imagined the whole thing, that she had been having a bad dream, but it was no dream. She could see the light under the door. He must still be in the flat. Did he intend to stay all night? He might change his mind later, come back... That would be unbearable. She slid out of bed and ran unsteadily to the door to bolt it, then leaned on it, trembling, the tears trickling down her white face.

How could he do that to her? She ran her hands angrily over her wet eyes, scrubbing out the tears. She would not cry for him. She hated him. She would never forgive him, never.

She heard a distant sound, and froze, listening— then identified it as someone running down the stairs. Was he leaving, after all? Then came the slam of a

heavy wooden door, and she recognised that too—
Ellis was leaving through the boathouse, not walking
up through the gardens. She went slowly over to the
window to look out, heard the sound of an engine
starting up, and a moment later saw a motor boat
slowly emerge below her and head up river. There were
lights in the cabin of the vessel; she had a brief glimpse
of black hair, oilskins, and then the boat was out of
sight around the bend, and silence descended once
more.

Claudia carefully unbolted her door and went out
to investigate. There was no sign of anyone now. She
went into the bathroom and washed her tear-stained
face, then went back to bed, but she didn't sleep. Her
mind churned with pain and anger all night, and in
the morning she went up to the house to breakfast,
prepared to face Ellis some time during the day, and
defy him.

She had dressed with great deliberation for the occasion, in a black jersey wool dress, her red-gold hair
swept up into a French pleat.

He didn't know that she was working for his father,
so no doubt he would return to the boathouse flat,
and when he saw all her possessions still around the
place, he would realise she had not left, as ordered,
but would he then come up to the house? When he
left for Japan, he had said he would be away for a
month, but he was back only two weeks later. Had
he come because Stephen rang him and said their
father wanted to see him? Or was it sheer coincidence
that had brought him back early?

Quentin raised his head as she entered the room,
and gave her his usual gruff, 'Morning, Claudia.'

'Good morning,' she said, sitting down opposite
him and grateful for once that he could not see her

face. Her voice sounded normal enough, but she knew she was pale and had shadows under her eyes.

Celeste came in with fresh coffee and stared with a frown as she poured Claudia a cup. 'You are not well?'

Quentin's head turned. 'What is that? Something wrong with the girl?'

'No,' Claudia said. 'I'm fine.'

'If you say so!' Celeste sniffed with disbelief.

'I didn't sleep very well, that's all,' Claudia insisted.

'A sleepless night usually means a man!' Celeste observed to nobody in particular, brushing invisible crumbs off the table.

'Well, this time it doesn't!' Claudia said fiercely.

'One of you tell me what is going on?' Quentin demanded of the air.

'It's nothing!' Claudia said.

'She's sickening for something, if you ask me, but apparently I am wrong, so excuse me...' Celeste went out, banging the door, and Quentin laughed, listening to her.

'She is offended.'

'I'm sorry,' Claudia said huskily, because a row with Celeste was the last straw, she couldn't cope with much more. She knew that any minute she would burst into tears.

Quentin shrugged. 'She offends easily! *Pas de problème*!' He returned to his croissant, dipping it into his hot chocolate and nibbling it with childish relish. 'Mmm . . . but she makes good croissants!'

Claudia took a roll and spread it with thick black cherry jam, which Celeste made herself each year. She wasn't hungry, though, so she sipped her strong coffee first, one eye on the window which looked over the gardens, down to the boathouse, watching on tenter-hooks for the first glimpse of Ellis.

'You know, if you would rather have an English breakfast, a bacon and egg, Celeste will cook it for you!' Quentin said abruptly, although when she first arrived he had made it clear that a Continental breakfast was all that was served in this house, and that she need not ask for anything else.

She looked at him in surprise, touched, because she knew it was a great concession and meant that he was getting to like her. 'Thank you, but Continental breakfast is what I'm used to!'

'Of course,' he grunted. 'I had forgotten—you have a French brother-in-law. A chef? Hmm...you are very lucky! Celeste's husband was a chef, did she tell you? She is a good cook, yes? But I think she would agree that her husband was better.'

'He must have been marvellous, then,' Claudia said, and Quentin smiled, as if she had paid him a compliment by praising Celeste.

'You like her cooking?'

'Very much. I'm sure Pierre, my brother-in-law, would be impressed by it, and you have to be good to impress Pierre. He thinks he is the best chef in the world.'

'All French chefs do!' Quentin drily commented.

Claudia was no longer listening. Tense and pale, she was staring out of the window. Ellis was striding up from the boathouse. He had changed into casual wear, English country clothes; a wax jacket, over a yellow polo-neck sweater, dark cord trousers. They suited him, he looked relaxed in them, from a distance, but when he got closer she saw that his brows were drawn angrily, his body tense. He had discovered that she had not moved out of the boathouse, and he was on his way here...to do what?

He was unaware that she worked for his father, so he would not expect to find her here, in this house. He had threatened to tell Quentin that Stephen was keeping a mistress in the boathouse—was that why he was here? Or was he merely here to see his father?

He had almost reached the house, she saw his face clearly, a brooding look on it, and began to get butterflies in her stomach. She quickly looked down at her coffee, lifted the cup to her lips with a hand that shook. There was an air of violence about him that made her very nervous. Surely, though, surely, he wouldn't risk having a quarrel with her in front of his father? She hated to imagine how Quentin would look if Ellis accused her of being Stephen's mistress. With anything like that, even if you proved yourself innocent, some mud was likely to stick; it might linger on in Quentin's mind—a question mark against her name.

A moment later, Quentin stiffened suddenly, his head lifted, listening. 'Who is Celeste talking to?'

Claudia couldn't hear anything, although she strained to pick up voices. Quentin's ears were much sharper than hers; he seemed able to hear like a bat, on a frequency way above that of most human beings.

His fingers tightened around his cup at that instant, and some coffee spilled on the polished surface of the table. He had turned pale.

The door opened, and Ellis came in briskly. His father turned towards the door, putting down his coffee-cup so suddenly that it rattled in the saucer. He waited, listening intently, then said with his usual impatience, 'Well! Who is it?'

Ellis didn't answer for a moment. He watched his father, his own face pale, too, and set in rigid lines, then his eyes flicked sideways and saw Claudia. He tensed, face tightening, but he did not look surprised. Had Celeste told him she was here? He looked far from pleased, however, but he needn't think that that bothered her. She did not either want, or need, his approval. She lifted her head in a defiant gesture and stared back, her green eyes bright with hostility.

Quentin had begun to frown, his forehead sharply corrugated. 'Claudia, who is it? What's going on? Tell me!'

'It's me, Papa,' Ellis said quietly, detaching his eyes from Claudia.

'Ah... Ellis... I thought I recognised that voice talking to Celeste,' Quentin breathed, then he frowned, and fell silent. 'Well, what are you doing here?' he muttered. 'I thought I told you never to set foot in this house again?'

'Do you want me to go?' Ellis bit out, his features angular and drawn, and Claudia could have hit him. Couldn't he see that his father's pride had made him say that? Quentin was afraid of admitting to any weakness; he would die rather than let Ellis know he had missed him. He wanted Ellis to humble himself, make all the overtures, so that he could make the magnificent gesture of forgiving him for whatever offence Ellis was supposed to have committed in the first place. It might be hard to swallow that attitude, and Ellis might have every right to resent it, but Quentin was an old man, and his father. Surely, Ellis could sacrifice his own pride this one time, and let Quentin win this battle?

'That's up to you!' Quentin said querulously, his blind stare turned away, then he burst out, 'I haven't set eyes on you for months, and, when you do show up here, you are offhand and hostile. Who do you think you are? What arrogance! I'm your father, damn you! Where is your respect? When I was your age, my father would have beaten me if I had spoken to him the way you speak to me! I suppose if I asked any questions about the way the business is going, I'd get my head bitten off! I don't have any right to know anything, I'm just your father. I was the man who built that corporation up over the years. It was my creation . . . But I'm old now, I must get out of the way, let you take over and I must not ask questions or want to know what you are doing . . .'

He broke off, his lower lip quivering as if he might be going to cry, and Claudia ran round the table to him and knelt beside his chair, taking his hand and holding it tightly, while she shouted at Ellis, 'Stop it! Can't you see what you're doing to him? You are the most selfish, self-obsessed man I've ever met. You have no decent impulses at all, do you? Whatever the wrongs and rights of the situation, he's your father, and he has been very ill. Tell him you're sorry, apologise . . .'

Ellis looked like a pillar of salt; not a muscle moved in his pale face, but there was icy hostility in his remote grey eyes as he stared at her. She had gone too far, been too brutally frank, he would never forgive her. For a moment she thought he would turn on his heel and walk out without a sound, but then he said stiffly, 'I apologise, Papa. I am very sorry if I have hurt you or upset you.'

Quentin drew a shaky breath, his cold, trembling fingers tightening around Claudia's hand.

'I am sorry, too...' he began, then broke off, holding out his free hand towards Ellis. *'Mon fils...'*

Ellis crossed the room in a rapid stride, bent and kissed his father on both cheeks, Gallic style. 'Papa! How are you? You look much better than you did the last time I saw you.'

Claudia freed herself and stood up, hurriedly moving away, back to her seat on the other side of the breakfast table. She found it disturbing to be too close to Ellis.

Quentin had more colour again; his face had re-laxed into easier lines. 'Ah,' he said cheerfully, 'That is due to this girl here ... my right hand! I don't know what I'd do without her, she's the first secretary I've had who had any brains or common sense. All her predecessors were vacuous, pin-brained females, who just agreed with everything I said, and cried if I so much as raised my voice to them. She's different, as you just saw.' He grinned, his blind eyes turned across the table to where she sat. 'She has a temper, and she says what she thinks. We argue like cat and dog, sometimes, but she has made it easier for me to get up in the mornings. I used to dread the day ahead, at one time, but not any more.'

Ellis was watching his father's face, his own taut and shaken. She knew his father so well now that it helped her to read Ellis's expressions, and she realised that it was a shock to him to realise how low Quentin had sunk over the past months, how deeply depressed he had become. He still was, of course; you could not expect an immediate cure. He was still given to dark moods, sudden rages, bleak depressions—but the patches of sunlight lasted longer all the time, the smiles came more frequently, he was beginning to make jokes.

'I'm sorry you've had such a bad time of it, Papa,' Ellis said slowly. 'Stephen didn't tell me it was so serious.' He paused, frowning. 'He did say you were very depressed,' he admitted. 'But I just did not understand, and I was so busy...'

Quentin's frown returned; there was petulance in the line of his mouth. Ellis had made a mistake by mentioning the corporation.

'Too busy to come and see your father!' he muttered. 'Well, I don't want to quarrel with you again—I won't ask any questions about the corporation...'

Claudia stared fixedly at Ellis, willing him to meet her eyes, and he turned his head to stare back at her. She gave a peremptory jerk of the head towards Quentin, then said aloud, 'I expect your son wants to consult you about some problem he has, sir, so I'll leave you two alone...'

'I doubt it,' Quentin said bleakly. 'You don't know him... I haven't introduced you, have I? Claudia, this is Ellis, my elder son, who is chairman and managing director of the corporation. Ellis, this is Claudia Thorburn.'

'We've met,' Ellis said curtly, and his father's face showed shock.

'What? When did you meet her? She never told me... I've often mentioned you, but she never said she knew you.' He turned his head in a gesture she found both familiar and poignant, his eyes straining in her direction, as if he still hoped he might suddenly be able to see her. 'Why didn't you say you knew him, Claudia? Very strange, that you do not say you know him. Why do you keep it to yourself?'

With a sinking heart, Claudia saw the flare of suspicion back in his face, heard the old note of sullen distrust in his voice. For a while, Quentin had been so much improved, so relaxed and cheerful, now he seemed to be back at square one. He was back where he had been when she first arrived; bleak, grim, remote, ready to see conspiracy behind everyday events, half paranoid, balanced on a mental knife edge.

'She does not like me,' Ellis said drily, staring across the room at Claudia, cold mockery in his face. He smiled, but he was not really amused. Not for the first time, Claudia saw a strong resemblance between the two men; a brooding, dark anger that disturbed her.

'Does not like you?' Quentin sounded incredulous, his eyebrows rising. 'I've never known a woman to dislike you.'

'This one does,' Ellis drily assured him.

'Claudia... Is he lying? Tell me, just between you and me,' murmured Quentin with amusement, 'do you like him?'

'No,' she said with force, and Ellis gave her a dark glowering stare.

Quentin laughed aloud. 'You see, Ellis—she isn't afraid to say what she thinks. I like that.'

'I can't say I do,' Ellis muttered. 'Some people might call it pure insolence!'

He gave her a pointed look and Claudia immediately said to his father, 'Your son is hinting that that was why I was sacked by the management of the hotel I worked for, sir. You remember, that was my last job before I came to work for you? You didn't bother to take up references for them because you had my agency reference, but the fact is, I was too frank with an important but very difficult guest. I was accused of insolence, and fired.'

Ellis eyed her menacingly, but she pretended not to be aware of that, lowering her lashes.

Quentin put his head on one side, grimacing. 'The difficult guest was a man, of course?'

'Yes, sir,' she said blandly.

'Ha.' He grinned. 'Some dull, middle-aged businessman who was away from his wife and family, and wanted a little fun? I can guess what happened, I think, oh, yes! He made advances to you?'

'Something like that, sir.' She ventured a glance at Ellis through her lashes and saw his profile, carved in flint, his mouth grim.

'And you turned him down?' Quentin slapped his knee, laughing. 'Good girl! I would like to have been there. I hope you slapped his face for him!'

'Father, I hate to interrupt,' said Ellis brusquely, 'but I can't stay long, and I would like the chance to talk to you in private.'

Smiling demurely, Claudia got up. 'Of course. Excuse me. I'll be in your study, if you need me, Mr Lefèvre.'

'I have left a tape on my desk for you,' he told her as she left. If Quentin could not sleep at night, he would sit up in bed, remembering his life and talking quietly into a dictaphone, as if he were reminiscing with an old friend. Claudia always enjoyed typing out those pages; they were immensely readable and had a casual, chatty style that he did not seem to achieve when he was dictating directly to her. Perhaps her presence inhibited him?

As she closed the door behind her, Celeste appeared, carrying a tray of fresh coffee and hot croissants, another cup, another plate and knife.

'*J'ai quelque chose pour M'sieur Ellis,*' she said happily, as Claudia glanced at the tray. '*Comment ça va? Vous pensez qu'il va bien?* They are not quarrelling?'

'Not yet,' Claudia said, opening the door again, to let her enter the room.

She went on to Quentin's study, but before she began work she rang Stephen in Cambridge. There was no reply from his flat and when she rang his laboratory she was told that he had not arrived yet. She left a message, asking him to ring her, and then she began to work on the material on Quentin's dictaphone. He spoke quite quickly but she was accustomed now to listening to him speak on tape, so she had no problem following what he said, and half an hour later she had several pages of the manuscript ready for Quentin. She was just coming to the end of last night's recording when the telephone rang.

'Oh, Stephen!' she said, on recognising the voice of the caller. 'Thank you for ringing back. Something has happened that I think you should know about. Your brother has turned up. He's with your father now.'

'What sort of mood are they in?' Stephen asked, sounding anxious, and he was right to feel that way. His father and brother were both difficult men.

'There was some friction at first,' she said slowly. 'Your father didn't want to admit he was pleased to see him, although he obviously was! He was grumpy and Ellis was touchy in his turn, you were quite right when you said that it was six of one and half a dozen of the other, and I told Ellis what I thought of him.'

'You did?' Stephen sounded amazed.

'Somebody had to say it! Your father is old, and living under the most enormous strain. Ellis isn't. Well, at least he seemed to listen, and they both made an effort to stop quarrelling, and I thought things looked quite promising, so I left them alone. It seemed a good idea at the time, to give them a chance to talk. I hope I did the right thing.'

'I'm sure you did!' said Stephen, but she was not reassured.

'But if anything went wrong, it could set your father back, just when he was making such good progress. Oh, I could kill your brother!'

'Would you like me to come over?' asked Stephen. 'I'm very busy at the moment, but if it would make you feel any easier?'

'Yes, it would, please come, Stephen,' she said, relief in her voice. 'I'll feel much better if you are here to deal with Ellis.'

'I'll come right away,' he promised, and rang off. She put the phone down, a smile still on her face, and heard a sound over by the door. Her head came up, her green eyes wide and startled. Ellis stood there, his face harsh, and her heart sank. He had heard everything she'd said.

CHAPTER SEVEN

'JUST what are you and my brother up to?' Ellis drawled icily, coming into the room and closing the door behind him. 'Why has he got you this job with my father?'

Claudia put both hands on the desk and faced him, her green eyes flashing with the hostility she felt whenever she saw him. She had never imagined that you could feel both such deep hostility and this terrible drag of attraction, but then she had never met anyone like Ellis Lefèvre before.

'I needed a job, remember! Because you lost me the last one.'

'Me? We had this argument before and I told you——'

'All right,' she interrupted. 'You—or your girl-friend—made sure I lost the last one.'

'So you asked my brother to find you one?' His black brows swooped upwards incredulously. 'Since when did Stephen set up to be an employment agency?'

'I didn't ask him. He suggested . . . he thought I might be able to get on with your father.'

'Oh, really? And what particular qualities did he feel you had?' Ellis asked bitingly, 'Apart from big green eyes, red hair and a sexy body?'

'Stephen doesn't have your one-track mind!' she burst out and he laughed coldly.

'He's a man, isn't he? Don't tell me he doesn't want you, because I wouldn't believe you. You may have been looking for a new job. OK. But what I want to know is why exactly did he bring you down here to work for my father? What was his motive? He must have one; nobody does anything without a reason.'

'He wanted to help me, that was his reason!' Claudia's voice rose angrily and he signalled with one hand in a peremptory gesture.

'My father will be coming along any minute, I left him talking to the gardener. Keep your voice down!'

'Why should I? I don't care if he hears me!'

She had hardly finished saying that when they both heard Quentin tapping his way along the corridor with his stick. He refused to have a guide dog. He had evolved his own way of getting about inside the house. Celeste never moved any furniture and Quentin had learnt every inch of the terraine in the house; he moved with his stick, feeling ahead of him to check exactly where he was at any given moment.

Claudia gave Ellis a triumphant, taunting smile. 'Unless you want to continue the discussion, I suggest you let me get on with my work, and you leave, before your father gets here.'

He gave her a look gleaming with menace, but didn't answer. Moving to the door, he opened it and said coolly, 'Ah, there you are, Papa. I was just going to set up that phone call for you. Thank you for helping me out of this difficulty. I was at my wits' end. Come and sit at your desk, and I'll dial the number.'

He moved to take his father's arm and Quentin nudged him out of the way with his elbow, shaking his head with a fiery look. 'I can find my own way, boy!'

Ellis fell back, picked up the telephone and began to dial. Quentin tapped his way to his chair and sank into it, leaning his stick beside it. He looked very cheerful, Claudia was relieved to see.

Ellis spoke in German into the telephone, then handed the phone to his father. 'Thank you, Papa,' he said, and Quentin nodded, smiling.

'Happy to help, my boy.'

Claudia wondered what exactly was going on, but she had no chance to find out because Ellis swung and grabbed her arm, jerking his head towards the door.

'This is strictly confidential, Miss Thorburn.'

Quentin held the phone in one hand, his head lifted sightlessly in their direction. 'Yes, Claudia, I am sorry... Would you mind leaving for a few moments?'

'Certainly, sir,' she said smoothly, collected her warm sheepskin jacket from a cupboard in the hall, and went out for a stroll in the garden. It was a cool February morning; the sky opalescent, soft blues and greys with a streak of gold where the sun lay behind a cloud.

Along the back wall of the house grew winter-flowering jasmine, bare, black branches gleaming with starry yellow flowers against the whitewashed stone. At this time of year there were almost no flowers around; the jasmine gave a splash of vivid colour to the garden. She lingered to pick a few branches for the vases in the hall, which Celeste liked to fill with flowers from their garden, or, if none was available, with branches of shrubs or grasses mixed with hot-house blooms grown in the greenhouse by the gardener. This jasmine was a useful stand-by since it flowered all through the winter and was so pretty.

Turning away, her arms full of the sprays of flowers, she found Ellis standing on the terrace, behind her, a few feet away, watching her, and her nerves prickled.

'Does your father want me?' she asked huskily, moving towards him.

'No, but I do,' he said with mockery edging his voice, and she tensed, her colour rising, but she refused to be taunted into answering him back this time. He might enjoy these barbed little exchanges, but she did not.

He was barring her way back to the house, and she wouldn't risk trying to pass him, so she turned away and walked down the steps into the garden, only to realise, too late, that that had been a bad move. Ellis followed her. She should have known he would.

She bit down on her inner lip. She had known. Of course she had. Walking away from the house instead of running to it, and to the safety of Celeste's protection, had been a Freudian slip, hadn't it? She hadn't done it deliberately, but she had known at the back of her mind that he would follow her if she came this way, yet she had come. What did that tell her about her state of mind?

'We hadn't finished our discussion,' he drawled, and she gave him an angry look.

'I had. I don't want to hear any more of your nasty, suspicious questions about your brother.' She halted, cradling the sprays of winter jasmine between them as if they were some sort of protection. Her angry green eyes roved over Ellis Lefèvre, from head to toe. 'Oh, it's impossible to believe that he's your brother. He's nothing like you, thank heavens. Stephen is kind and thoughtful, and I know I can trust him.'

Ellis laughed shortly. 'But you don't trust me?'

'No, I don't.' She made no attempt to soften that retort and Ellis watched her, his grey eyes hard and glittering.

'Is Stephen your lover?' he suddenly bit out.

'No, he is not!' she threw back with a similar force. 'I told you that last night!'

'Last night I was too angry to listen,' he said flatly. 'When I found you there, in the boathouse flat, I jumped to the conclusion that Stephen had installed you there, and was visiting you secretly, without my father knowing anything about it. Celeste would have to know; nothing happens here without Celeste knowing, but she always kept our secrets when we were young. She wouldn't tell, and my father never goes down there. He wouldn't be able to see you coming and going, although he might hear something, if he came down the garden.' He drew a rough breath, shrugging. 'I was so furious when I saw you that my imagination ran riot, picturing you and Stephen together. I couldn't think rationally, but in the morning light it seems so unlikely.'

Flushed, she said in contrary pique, 'What—that Stephen might want me?'

His eyes gleamed through their black lashes, and his smile was infuriatingly amused. She could have kicked herself for letting her ego betray her. 'Oh, no, that is only too likely!' he murmured, as his eyes moved slowly, caressingly, over her from her red-gold head to her long, slender legs. 'But that isn't the question. Do you want him? That is what I wasn't sure about, but this morning I can't believe it for an instant.'

She couldn't meet his eyes, and she did not like the smile she heard in his voice, so she bent to breathe in the scent of the yellow jasmine, the flowers brushing her cheek.

'No comment?' he murmured. 'I'll take that for an admission, you know.'

She gave him a brief, irritated look. 'I kept telling you last night that there was nothing going on between me and Stephen, but you were in such a nasty temper that you wouldn't believe me.'

He was silent for a moment then with obvious reluctance, said: 'Oh, OK, I was jealous...'

Her heart missed a beat. She kept her eyes down, but she was listening with intensity, hardly able to believe what he was saying.

'I couldn't think straight,' he muttered. 'I was too furious with you for choosing Stephen instead of me... For some reason, that really hurt. Any other man might not have been so bad, but my brother! I couldn't stand the idea of that.'

Because his father preferred his brother? wondered Claudia suddenly. Of course—Ellis must resent the fact that his father had refused to see him, yet was always happy to see Stephen. That was enough to make anyone jealous; she knew she would have been jealous herself if her parents had played her off against Annette; but luckily they had been careful never to have favourites. Family quarrels were always the most bitter and divisive, had the most lasting effects. This one would be complicated by the fact that Ellis and his father were so alike; they had the same forceful, obstinate natures. They could hurt each other more, know just where to hit to hurt most.

Ellis grimaced. 'And, in any case, Stephen just isn't the type to bring his girlfriend down here and use our father's home as a love-nest. I must have been crazy to think he would.' He paused, then said roughly,

'And I was, of course... Quite crazy, at that moment, with jealousy...'

She hoped he could not hear the beating of her heart; it was almost deafening her.

'I believe you now,' Ellis finished wryly, glancing sideways at her, his mouth crooked, and she looked at him through her lashes, feeling a queer, protective sympathy for the pain he must have felt over his father's rejection of him. How could one blame Quentin, though? In his situation, fighting his slowly increasing blindness, filled with despair and rage, he hadn't really known what he was doing. He was too unhappy himself to realise what he was doing to his elder son; he had only known that Ellis had supplanted him in running the corporation, and he wasn't rational enough, in his pain, to be able to recognise that it was fate, not Ellis himself, which had dealt that blow.

Quentin had probably always been fonder of Stephen than of his elder son, because the younger boy took after his mother, but when Ellis had taken over the corporation, Quentin's preference had deepened, and darkened, until he had shut out Ellis altogether. What a painful muddle it was, thought Claudia; Quentin had been jealous of Ellis, who in turn had been jealous of his brother. Until now, it hadn't really dawned on her that the same bitter feelings churned around in them both.

Perhaps, now that they had made some sort of tentative approach to each other, they could actually talk it out and start to understand each other?

'Well, I'm glad you've sorted that out,' she said gently, and ambiguously, and turned back towards the house. 'Now, I had better get back before your father starts calling for me.'

'He will be on the phone for another half an hour at least.' Ellis put a hand under her arm and steered her towards the river, round the boathouse, on to the path along the riverbank, where bare willows hung towards the grey water and a covey of ducks quacked in alarm, and waddled hurriedly away from the human intruders into their domain, then swam in circles, waiting to see if there was any food coming.

There was a white-painted Victorian ironwork bench nearby. 'Let's sit and watch the river,' Ellis said, and Claudia could not think of a reason why they shouldn't, so she sat down and he sat beside her, turning to face her, one leg crossed over the other, his arm along the back of the bench.

'I thought we were going to watch the river,' Claudia said tartly, fixing her own eyes on the gleaming water. 'We mustn't stay long. Your father is going to send out search parties soon.' It made her intensely nervous to have him so close, watching her.

'He has too much to do to think about you. We've run into problems with our German subsidiary, and my father is sorting things out. That's why I flew back from Tokyo, why I'm here—I wouldn't have felt I had to come back if we hadn't got serious trouble. I shall have to go there myself, I would have left today, but it will be an enormous help if, first of all, my father can talk things out with the German management.'

'I see,' she said, not sure she did, and Ellis gave her an amused smile, reading her perplexed expression.

'The point is, my father set the company up, he has known the German managing director for years. They are old friends, and of the same generation. The man will talk more openly with my father than he probably would to me.'

Claudia's green eyes searched his face, she was frowning thoughtfully. 'Do you run into that problem often? Corporation executives who would rather deal with your father?'

His grey eyes were sharp and narrowed, a flicker of irritation in his face. 'Occasionally I do—it's only to be expected. Some of the older men resent the change at the top. They would resent me, whoever I was. The status quo is always more comforting than change of direction.' He frowned at her. 'I don't have to remind you not to repeat what I've said to my father, do I? I don't want him worrying about this. I can cope with it. In any case, in time, the old guard will retire and the problem won't exist any more.'

'You haven't told your father, then?' she slowly said, and he scowled, brows black.

'No, I just said... I don't want him worrying about it!'

'Don't you think he might be able to help? As he is now, for instance? Acting as a bridge between you and these men?'

'I can't ask him to do that!' he muttered, an irritated tic beating beside his mouth.

'You've asked him this time!'

'This time is different; it was urgent... There's a strike brewing, and a row between the members of the German board of directors... I wasn't quite sure what was going on, but I had to get it settled fast because we have a vital contract to fulfil, and I hoped my father could succeed where I was failing——' He broke off, looking exasperated. 'Why am I telling you all this? It means nothing to you.'

'I understand that you needed your father,' she said quietly. 'And I know how much that will mean to him. Can't you put yourself in his place? Blind, ill, shutting himself up here away from everybody? How do you think he's been feeling?'

'That's precisely why I don't want to worry him! I know he has had a very bad time these last two years. I've tried to lift as much from his shoulders as I could.'

'You don't think he might feel excluded?' she said softly, and Ellis gave her a hard, frowning stare.

'Do you think he does? He has never said anything to me . . .'

'Except to forbid you to visit him,' Claudia said and Ellis's eyes flashed angrily.

'So. Who told you that? Stephen, I suppose? I don't like the idea of my private life being discussed with all and sundry. I'll have a few words to say to him when I see him.'

'While you're busy nursing your own ego, you might spare a thought for your father's!' Claudia burst out, and he stiffened with affront. She didn't care how angry he was, she had to make him see the truth. 'Being blind hasn't made him mentally incapable, you know. He still has all his other faculties. He's a very clever, very shrewd man, and he's full of energy, but it has all been building up inside him, with nowhere to go. I think the idea of writing his own life story has helped. He's enjoying remembering, making notes, starting files on people and events. He is very organised. We spend hours with reference works, checking up on the people he has known, to make sure his memory isn't at fault. But he still gets frustrated and angry about being shut out of all the corporation business.'

'I don't shut him out! When I took over, around two years ago, he was very ill, you know. Did Stephen explain that? He had a minor stroke, he had raging blood-pressure and his heart wasn't too good, either. The blindness was a slower process; I think it had probably caused the blood-pressure and the stroke, because he was refusing to admit that his sight was going. He had to stop working, and I was thrust into this job. I didn't ask for it—my father told me to take over. His doctors asked me never to discuss business with him. They said it might cause a relapse, so I took their advice, and my father resented it. That was when he ordered me out of the house, and told me he never wanted to see me again.'

'That must have hurt you badly,' Claudia said, her green eyes full of sympathy.

He nodded in bleak silence, staring at the river. For a moment they sat in silence, then Claudia said, 'When you turned up last night, I assumed Stephen had rung you and asked you to come back and see your father because he was asking for you.'

'I rang Stephen in London, yesterday evening, as soon as I got back from Tokyo,' Ellis said, his brows together in a heavy frown. 'Stephen told me he thought I wouldn't get thrown out if I came down here. He told you about that, too, did he? I suppose he hasn't told you about my birthmark, and all my girlfriends too? Is there anything in my private life that you haven't heard about? Do the two of you ever talk about anything else?'

Claudia smiled at his glowering expression. 'Have you got a birthmark? Where? Stephen forgot to mention that.'

He stopped scowling, and his eyes gleamed with sudden amusement. 'I'll be only too happy to show you some time,' he mocked, and watched the faint pinkness invade her face.

'Anyway,' she hurriedly said, looking away, 'I'm very discreet, you don't need to be afraid I'll repeat anything—I told you that the first time we met! In fact, your father told *me* that he missed you, he didn't tell Stephen. It was actually me who asked your brother to get in touch with you and pass the message on——'

Her words broke off in startled surprise as Ellis suddenly caught her face in both hands, turning it up towards him. Her green eyes widened, the pupils black and dilated, staring at him with an apprehension which was half excitement. Ellis looked down into her face, his palms warm on her cheeks, his fingertips pressing softly on her temples.

'So it was you, was it? I might have known. I can see my father thinks the sun shines out of you. He kept telling me you were a terrific secretary, and what a sharp little wasp you were, how you snap right back at him if he snaps at you. That seems to impress him a great deal, far more than all your amazing efficiency.'

'I think he was bored with people being sweetness and light to him, and ignoring his bad temper and sulks,' Claudia explained. 'Stephen had warned me to be patient with him, and I was, at first, until it dawned on me that he was just irritable because he was so bored.'

'And now he's eating out of your hand?'

She laughed. 'Oh, I wouldn't say that! Your father is not an easy man to deal with. But we get on much better these days.'

'And you talked him into sending for me?' Ellis smiled down into her eyes. 'For his sake—or yours? Did you miss me?'

Flushed, she gave him a furious look. 'No, I didn't! I didn't talk your father into anything. He said he wanted to see you, that's all.'

'And you didn't?' he teased, then his head came down and his mouth lightly brushed her lips, whispering against them, 'Sure about that?'

Claudia tried to draw back her head, and his hand slid round, stroking her hair, to clamp the back of her head and make sure she could not pull far away from him.

'You're beautiful, you know that, don't you?' he said softly, and then he kissed her with a passion which swallowed her like a great wave, so that she drowned in it, unable to see or hear anything else, clinging to him to save herself, her arms going round his neck, holding on to him tightly, her body swaying towards him like tendrils of weed flowing with a tide they could not resist.

When he stopped kissing her it was like being broken out of a trance; she was disorientated, confused, her colour high, her breathing rapid.

Ellis was breathing fast, too, his eyes like burnished steel, brilliant and dangerous. He ran his fingers over her red-gold hair, smiling crookedly.

'A pity I have to be off to Germany tonight. When I get back, can we have dinner in town? I'll ring and make a firm date when I know what I'm doing.'

'I only go into town at weekends,' she said huskily, and Ellis gave her an amused smile.

'Oh, I think we can persuade my father to let you have an evening off to meet me.' He glanced at his watch and sighed, releasing her and sitting up. 'We had better get back, I suppose! He must be off the phone by now. Let's hope he managed to work something out.' He got to his feet and Claudia stood up, too, a little weak at the knees but trying to hide it.

'I thought you liked to be in the centre of London so that you could get to auditions if one came up suddenly?' Ellis asked as they walked back to the house. 'Isn't it a problem for you, living out here?'

'I had a morning off one week for an audition,' she said, shrugging. 'But nothing interesting has come up since I started work here. I've managed to get weekend appointments with my voice coach—on Saturday mornings. And I go to the gym at weekends, too, and keep up my exercises on my own here before I go down to breakfast.'

He gave her a thoughtful look. 'You went to drama school, I remember—did you ever have any success?'

Slightly defensive, she gave him the highlights of her career, then in a fit of honesty said, 'I know I'm not ever going to be a star, but I love acting.'

'You should aim for television or film,' Ellis said, considering her face and figure with amused eyes. 'You must be very photogenic. Have you got an agent? He isn't doing much of a job, is he?'

'He has a lot of much more successful clients,' she wryly said.

They went back into the house, but, before they rejoined Quentin, Ellis said, 'When we meet in London, would you like me to get tickets for a play, instead of just having dinner? We could have supper after the theatre.'

'Yes, please,' she said eagerly. 'I used to go to the theatre several times a week, at least, until I started working out here. I do miss it.'

'OK,' Ellis said, turning towards the door of his father's study, but before he opened it they both heard the front doorbell ringing, and Celeste grumblingly going to open it.

Stephen? thought Claudia ruefully, wishing now that she had not rung him in such a panic and asked him to come down here. Her wild visions of what Ellis might plan to do to her had not come true, thank heavens.

Ellis gave her a sideways glance, lifting one black brow. 'Can this be my dear brother. Come hotfoot from London to rescue you from me?' The mockery in his voice made her go pink, laughing.

Then they heard the new arrival's voice, and realised that it was not Stephen. Claudia stopped laughing. She knew that voice. It was Estelle's.

Shooting a hurried look at Ellis, she saw that his face had gone blank, his lids half down over his grey eyes. Had he asked Estelle to join him here? He must have done. Why else would she be here? She hadn't visited Quentin before, she couldn't have come to see him. She was here to see Ellis, which meant that he had wanted to see her.

Celeste appeared, mouth rigid. 'Ellis, you have a visitor,' she began, but Estelle was right behind her, and did not wait for Celeste to finish. She flew past the housekeeper and stood on tiptoe to kiss Ellis on his mouth.

'Oh, darling, I've missed you... It seems years since I saw you...'

Claudia was sick with jealousy. She tried to look away but couldn't; she had to know the truth. She watched them with strained attention, trying to work out how Ellis really felt about Estelle, but it was impossible to tell because he knew she was there, watching him.

It was easy to guess how Estelle felt about him. She made no secret of it, kissing him lingeringly, her arms clasping his neck, her body leaning towards him in yearning. She couldn't have been more obvious if she had tried, Claudia thought sourly.

Ellis deftly managed to free himself without difficulty—Claudia wasn't even sure how he had done it. One minute he was wreathed with Estelle—the next he wasn't. Cleverly done, she thought. How often has he used that trick? She mustn't forget that there had been plenty of other women before her. Did she want to be one in a long line? How many would there be after her? That was the real question, and she felt a black depression coming down on her as she faced that one. She couldn't trust him to be faithful, could she? Nobody could. It would be pure crazy folly if you did.

Estelle didn't seem worried by the way he had wriggled out of her grasp, though. She went on smiling at him, smoothing down her brunette hair with one slim, pale hand. She was as elegant and expensively dressed as she had been when Claudia met her in London. Today, she wore a flame-red wool dress, under a black mink jacket, and looked a million dollars. Easy for her, Claudia thought, when her father was worth millions. Try looking that way on an ordinary working girl's salary!

'I know you said you'd see me at the airport tonight, but I couldn't wait,' Estelle said throatily. 'I had to see you sooner than that. You don't mind, do you, darling? I haven't seen your father for ages, I thought it would be nice to visit him, while you're here, and then we could drive back to London together to catch our plane. I suppose I shouldn't say this, but I'm hoping it is going to take you days to fix this German problem, and we can have lots of time together before you have to dash off to Tokyo again.'

She was going to Germany with him, Claudia thought, the pain of the realisation almost more than she could bear. He had come down here and made love to her, made a date with her to meet in London when he got back, and all the time he had had another woman waiting for him in London, and was planning to take her with him on his business trip.

Ellis shot her a look, frowning, and she held herself stiffly, trying to hide the cold whiteness of her skin, the shadowed look in the green eyes. He had made a fool of her, lied to her, but somehow she would retrieve some sort of dignity—she would not let him see just how badly he had hurt her.

CHAPTER EIGHT

ESTELLE had noticed that she didn't have Ellis's attention; she looked round to see what he was staring at, and saw Claudia with an audible intake of breath, turning a rather nasty shade of red, which, Claudia smugly felt, did not suit her, especially in that dress!

'What's she doing here?' she demanded, looking Claudia up and down very rudely.

'She works for my father,' Ellis said in a clipped way, deliberately offhand.

'You got her a job with your father?' Estelle apparently could not believe her ears. Had she ordered him not to see Claudia again?

'No, I didn't!' Ellis said irritably. 'It was my brother Stephen's idea; he knew my father needed a secretary, and he introduced her to Papa. I only found out about it today.'

'Do you expect me to believe that?' Estelle shrilled, and Ellis flinched, looking grim, and yet hunted at the same time. Estelle probably had that effect on a lot of people, but Claudia felt no sympathy for his plight. He wouldn't stand up to Estelle, she was certain of that, and she decided that she was not waiting around to hear him apologise for her presence in his father's house.

She was both angry and miserable, and afraid that at any minute she was going to burst into tears, so she walked away, very fast, and went into his father's study where the old man was just putting down the telephone. He turned his head, smiling, knowing her step by now. His hearing was amazingly acute, and growing more so every day, she felt.

'Ah! Claudia! Where is my son? I have much news for him.' His accent was decidedly German today, she noted, after that long discussion on the phone. She was able to find a faint, weary amusement in that. He was vocally a chameleon, taking on the accent of any language he had just been speaking. At times she was convinced he had been born English, at others that he was a French native, and his Italian was amazing, too, but then she knew he had worked all over Europe.

Stephen said that Ellis had inherited his father's linguistic talent, and Stephen himself certainly spoke the main European languages fluently. They had had the advantage of being taught by special tutors from an early age, of course, but still she admired their ability, and envied it. When she was living in central London again, she was determined to start taking lessons at a language school, and broaden her linguistic horizon.

'Your son is talking to a friend outside, he should be here soon,' she said huskily. She tried hard to sound perfectly normal, but Quentin must have picked up something in her voice, because he frowned.

'Is anything wrong, Claudia?'

'No, nothing, I'm fine,' she said hurriedly. 'I finished work on your tape, you know. Have you got anything else for me to do, or don't you need me while your son is here this morning?'

She was hoping that he would tell her to take the morning off—she wanted to get away and stay away until Ellis had left—but she spoke very quietly, because she didn't want Ellis to hear her ask his father to let her go, especially as she could hear them, now, right outside the door, could hear Estelle talking fast and furiously in that light, high voice, scolding Ellis, who listened in silence.

'Who is that angry woman?' Quentin asked uncertainly. 'I don't recognise the voice.' He listened in frowning disbelief for a while, trying to place it, then said, 'It isn't Estelle Harding, is it? I think it is! Why is she lecturing Ellis like that?'

No doubt, thought Claudia grimly, she is ordering him to talk to his father about me, tell him that I'm not a suitable secretary, I'm insolent and I don't just melt into the wallpaper, as a good secretary should! Ellis wasn't arguing over that; he wasn't saying anything, he was just listening, letting Estelle do all the talking. That might indicate discretion, or cowardice—or perhaps he would rather she didn't work for his father, for his own reasons?

Maybe I'm going to get fired again, thought Claudia defiantly, but determined not to let it break her heart. Ellis hadn't done anything about getting her back her job at the hotel, had he? If he let his girlfriend engineer her dismissal from this job, he was beneath contempt.

She was fond of Quentin, and she liked living in the flat over the boathouse; it was wonderful to have so much room to herself, to be so independent, and she liked being by the river and watching it in all its changing moods, but at this precise moment she longed to be back in central London, with her own family around her, supporting her. She wanted to escape from this emotional minefield, where at any moment something might blow up in her face and wreck her life. All she wanted was to find some sort of peace, achieve stability, stop see-sawing up and down between such extremes of mood. The last time she could remember feeling like this was as a teenager, and she had no wish to go back to that disturbed and disturbing period of her life. She had thought that all that was far behind her, but here it was again, like a recurring nightmare.

'I suppose it is a lovers' tiff,' Quentin thought aloud, pulling a droll face. 'She scolds him as if they had been married twenty years! Ellis is not going to marry her, is he?'

Claudia pretended not to have heard that question. She sat down at her own desk and switched on her screen, pretended to be studying the text she had keyed in earlier.

'Shall I read this new passage to you?' she asked Quentin, who looked confused.

'What?' He was still eavesdropping on his son's quarrel with Estelle.

'The tape you left me... I've put it on disk—you may want to change a few things, shall I read it out?'

'Ah, yes. Good, yes, do that.' Quentin put his fingertips together, forehead wrinkling as he listened to her reading. 'Yes, that sounds good, don't you agree?'

'Definitely,' she said, half distracted by the sounds outside the door.

'Then I won't revise it. Add it to the rest of the material.' Quentin chuckled. 'The manuscript must be growing quite thick by now.'

'It is,' she agreed, picking up the pages and weighing them in her hands, then she stiffened as the door opened and Ellis came into the room alone.

Quentin picked up his arrival at once, of course, turning to gaze blindly in that direction. 'Ellis?'

Ellis didn't answer for a second, staring instead at her, across the study, grey eyes insistently trying to make her look back at him, but Claudia kept on staring at the screen in front of her, pretending to be absorbed.

'Who is it? Ellis, is that you?' Quentin queried and his son had to answer him, his voice slow and abstracted.

'Yes, Papa.'

'Who have you been talking to out there? It wasn't Estelle Harding?'

'Yes, it was, Papa.' Ellis still hadn't taken his eyes from Claudia, and she was still ignoring him.

'Where is she?' Quentin turned his head from side to side, as if trying to pick up some sound from Estelle. He held out his hand, smiling politely. 'Estelle ... How are you, my dear?'

'She isn't here, Papa,' Ellis said quickly. 'I wanted to talk to you alone.'

'Ah,' said Quentin, letting his hand drop. 'Is she outside?'

'No, Papa, she has left the house.'

Claudia risked a quick look at Ellis, hearing that, but his face was as bland and unreadable as his voice. She wondered if his quarrel with Estelle had been serious—who had won? What significance did Estelle's departure have? She couldn't tell by watching Ellis.

Quentin made a wry little face, looking serious. 'Well, so long as she is not here, my boy, I can be frank. You know I never interfere in your private life, either yours or Stephen's. But I must say I was amazed to hear Estelle talking to you just now. Does she always nag you like that? I had no idea she was so ferocious. Just like her mother, mind you. I remember Enid when she was young—very beautiful, and full of energy, but so domineering. Before you propose to any woman, my boy, take a look at her mother! It can usually tell you what you will get in twenty years' time!'

'I'll bear that in mind, Papa,' Ellis coolly said, walking over to sit on his father's desk, swinging those long legs of his.

'Do, my boy, do.' Quentin tilted back his head, noting that his son's voice came from closer at hand. 'Now, don't you knock anything off my desk! I have to know where everything is, don't I, Claudia?'

'Yes, sir,' she said coolly, knowing that Ellis was still staring at her, and averting her own eyes.

'Oh, I'm very careful,' Ellis said.

Claudia was quite sure of that! He had been very careful about keeping Estelle away from here. It wasn't his fault that she had arrived, blowing all his little plans to smithereens. If it hadn't been for that, Claudia would be in heaven right now, looking forward to meeting him when he got back from Germany, and no doubt gazing at him, wide-eyed with excitement, while he smiled at her, knowing that his blind father could not see either of them.

'Well, Papa?' he said now, briskly, in his business-like tones, 'How did you get on with Ernst?'

'He was glad to have a chance to put his side of it to me, he was very frank.' Quentin paused, chewing his lower lip, swivelling his head in her direction, the wintry sunlight striking on his lids and giving him the look of a weatherbeaten stone statue with carved eyes. 'Claudia, I'm sorry, my dear, but this is very confidential...'

She immediately got up. 'Of course, sir, I'll go and see if Celeste needs any help.'

Quentin looked dubious, knowing Celeste's dislike of having any other female in her kitchen. 'Well... Hmm...'

'Or I might just get some coffee,' Claudia suggested tactfully, making him smile. 'Would you like some?'

'Please,' Quentin said. 'I've been talking so much, my throat is as dry as dust.'

She avoided Ellis's glance and walked to the door, conscious of his eyes on her at every step, and resenting it. He had almost fooled her; she could kick herself for being taken in like that! Had she really been crazy enough to believe, even for an instant, that he was serious about her? Her face burned with humiliation as she suddenly remembered how happy she had been a few moments before Estelle arrived.

How could she have forgotten her doubts about him when, right from the start, her common sense had warned her that a man as rich and powerful as Ellis Lefèvre would only have one reason for taking an interest in her—he just wanted to get her into bed?

She had been around; you couldn't live in the West End of London, and move in theatrical circles, without becoming pretty sophisticated. She had had boyfriends, she knew the score where most men were concerned. So why had Ellis Lefèvre managed to convince her just now that he was different?

Her mouth twisted in self-contempt. Well, obviously—her unconscious had wanted to be deceived, of course; she had been eager to believe it. She had been falling for Ellis long before that walk down to the river this morning. She had been an easy target for his particular brand of guerrilla warfare because she was half in love with him already.

Half in love? she bitterly queried as she went into the kitchen. Rather more than half, wasn't it? Damn him.

'*Qu'est-ce que vous dites?*' Celeste asked, lifting a flushed face from the oven in which she was cooking *boeuf en daube*; a rich, heavy casserole of beef in a big casserole dish. The smell pervaded the entire kitchen; vinous, delicious, and one of Quentin's favourite meals.

'I was talking to myself, that's all,' Claudia muttered, appalled to think that she had been talking aloud—how much had Celeste heard, for heaven's sake? Hurriedly, she added, 'Quentin wants coffee… I'll make it, don't worry.'

Celeste fanned her hot face with a tea towel. '*Merci, mais c'est presque prêt…*' she said tartly, gesturing to a tray on which stood a coffee pot and several cups, sugar bowl, cream jug. 'I was just going to bring it in!'

'They don't want me in there; will you take it in? They're having a confidential discussion. Can I have a cup of your own coffee?'

'*Servez-vous!*' Celeste shrugged, making for the door, and Claudia picked up the battered French enamelled coffee-pot which always stood on the old range Celeste still preferred to use instead of the elaborate and expensive ovens standing side by side with it in the ultra-modern kitchen. Celeste liked her coffee thick, strong and sweet, which was just how Claudia needed it at that moment.

She was sitting at the kitchen table, drinking her coffee, ten minutes later, when Stephen arrived, his hair windblown and his face urgent after a very fast drive down the motorway from Cambridge.

She had heard his car arrive, peered out and recognised him, so she met him at the front door. He
looked down at her, his brown eyes anxious. 'Is
everything OK? My father...'

'He's fine,' she reassured him, feeling guilt-stricken
because she had forgotten asking him to come at once
to deal with Ellis. It seemed such a long time ago, so
much had happened since then. 'Oh, Stephen, I'm
sorry, I've wasted your time; you need not have come
at all, nothing has happened, they are getting on well
and, in fact, your father is enjoying himself enor-
mously. At first, it did seem as if they were going to
fight, though, and I'm afraid I panicked. Stupid of
me. I am sorry.'

Stephen let his shoulders slacken, sighing. 'Oh,
that's OK, don't worry about it. I'd much rather you
erred on the side of caution, and with those two, anything could have happened!' He followed her through
the house to the kitchen, sniffing. 'Coffee? Is there
any left? I'm dying for some.'

She poured him a cup and he held it in both hands,
nursing it, leaning against the wall. 'That smells delicious. Where are they now, by the way?'

'In your father's study. There's some sort of crisis
going on in Germany and your brother came to ask
your father for help and advice.'

Stephen's brows shot up in astonishment. 'He did?'

'He didn't tell you, when you talked on the phone,
last night, that he meant to do that?'

'We didn't discuss the business, we never do. I op-
erate on an entirely different wavelength from my
brother.' Stephen's tone was dry. 'Which is probably
just as well, because if we were rivals it could get very
nasty. Ellis is a competitive animal; he likes to win

any contest he enters, and I doubt if he would use kid gloves just because I was his brother.'

Claudia didn't think it wise to comment on that; she was sure Stephen was a hundred per cent accurate but it was not a good idea to agree with him, she felt.

'That isn't why you became a scientist instead of going into the business side of the corporation?' she asked him curiously, and he shook his head, face wry.

'Oh, no, I wanted to be a scientist! It wasn't just cowardice.' He grinned at her. 'I'm not sure if I would back off from an out and out conflict with Ellis—I've often wondered if I would. Just between you and me, I do find my big brother intimidating. So far, though, we haven't had to fight over anything important to either of us, but I'm glad that we don't ever fancy the same woman! I'd hate to think what Ellis would do to me if he thought I wanted his girl!'

Claudia looked out of the window and watched the distant grey gleam of the river. The sun had gone in and the view was bleak.

Stephen finished his coffee and put the cup down. 'Well, I'll go and say hello! Does he know I'm coming, by the way?'

'Yes.' Claudia didn't tell him how Ellis had reacted to the news. She wasn't sure what sort of reception he would get, but in front of their father no doubt Ellis would be friendly enough. 'I'll come too,' she decided. 'They have probably finished their confidential discussion by now.'

As they arrived at the study, they heard Quentin laughing, and the deep, amused tones of Ellis's voice, and Stephen paused to look down at her in surprised pleasure. 'My father sounds almost like his old self! You've worked a miracle, Claudia!'

'Not me,' she said. 'Ellis. Your father was so happy to be asked to help him! I think, you know, that that is what he really needs—to get involved in the corporation again. I can't see why being blind should be an obstacle. If he has a secretary he can trust, to read everything to him, he can deal with almost any situation. It's just a matter of confidence.'

'You're right, of course, but when he stopped work it wasn't so much because of his sight as because of his state of mind. He was very ill, he couldn't cope with a tough job at the time. Has he talked to you about it, then?'

She shook her head. 'Not exactly, but I think he would jump at the chance to go back.'

'I'll mention it to him, while Ellis is here, and see what they both say.' Stephen opened the door and stood back to let her walk into the room. Ellis and his father stopped talking; Ellis looked quickly at Claudia, who kept her eyes down and walked over to her desk.

'It's me, Father,' Stephen said and his father's face lit up with that special smile he kept for his younger son. He held out a blue-veined hand and Stephen went over to clasp it and bend to kiss his father on both cheeks in the usual ritual French kiss.

'I wasn't expecting you!' said Quentin.

'I came down because Ellis told me he would be here, and I thought it would be nice to make it a real family occasion. It's a long time since we were all together. How about the three of us going out for lunch?'

'I don't think I'll have time,' Ellis said flatly.

'Make time!' Quentin ordered in a smiling tone. 'I think it's a very good idea. Where shall we go?'

'I'll book a table at that Italian restaurant you always liked, Papa. Can I use your phone?'

Stephen took a little black diary from the inside pocket of his jacket and flicked through the pages, then dialled a number and began speaking in fluent Italian.

Under cover of his brother's voice, Ellis stepped closer to Claudia and asked softly, 'Are you coming?'

She shook her head, not looking at him. 'This is a family affair.'

He turned his back on his father and bent towards her, his lips barely moving as he murmured, 'I want to see you alone before I have to leave.'

'I don't want to see you,' she whispered back, hoping his father's quick ears couldn't pick up what they were saying.

'Claudia, at least listen to me!' he muttered thickly, but she shook her head, face cold, and at that instant Stephen put the phone down and turned round, smiling.

'We have a table for one o'clock, so we'll have to go at once, OK? Then we can have a quiet talk, just the three of us, about the future.'

Quentin looked startled, his grizzled brows rising. 'The future? Stephen, you aren't about to break some news to us, are you? Is this the girl you were telling me you liked so much?'

Stephen looked confused and turned pink. 'Did I?'

His father eagerly asked, 'You aren't going to get married, are you?'

Ellis stiffened, his eyes fixed on Claudia, who was pretending to be very busy tidying the drawers of the desk.

She met that stare, her face remote, almost hating him for the way he was looking at her. She knew the conclusion he had immediately jumped to; she read the jealousy in his eyes, and knew it was real. He was too angry for it to be fake. But Ellis wasn't in love with her. He just wanted her, and that was hardly flattering. If she slept with him, he would soon get bored and forget her, but because she kept rejecting him he was frustrated and angry, and he hated the thought of any other man in her life, especially his own brother.

Stephen said offhandedly, 'Married? Me? Whatever put that idea into your head? No, I just had a suggestion to put to you, about the corporation.'

Ellis took his eyes away from Claudia, slowly, and gave his brother a wintry stare, face hard. 'About the corporation? Since when did you interest yourself in the business side?'

'Never mind that now, I'd much rather talk about it over lunch—it isn't something for a snap decision. Come on, Ellis, say you'll come.'

'If you're going to talk about the corporation, I'd better be there, hadn't I?' Ellis bit out, and the hostility in his tone made Quentin frown with uneasiness.

'Stephen will be a major shareholder one day; he has a right to an opinion about the corporation!' he said sharply.

'It doesn't matter, Papa, leave it,' Stephen hurriedly said. 'You'll come out to lunch with me, won't you?'

Quentin nodded. 'I would be happy to.' He was still frowning in Ellis's direction, his face stern.

'We might as well all go in one car, then,' said Stephen. 'Shall we take mine?'

'You take Papa,' said Ellis. 'I'll go in my own car, because afterwards I must drive on to London straight away. I'm off to Germany early this evening.'

Quentin got up, feeling for his stick. 'I will go and get ready, then. I won't be long, Stephen. Claudia, tell Celeste I need her in my bedroom, will you?'

She hurried away and sent Celeste up to him at once, lingering in the kitchen to avoid running into Ellis again. Stephen joined her a few moments later. He was flushed and excited.

'I'll get some wine into them before I tackle the subject of my father going back to work. Did you get the impression Ellis was going to be difficult? Do you think he guessed what I was going to suggest? He's amazingly quick to pick up ideas, even shadows of ideas! That's probably why he's so good at running the corporation. I'm sure I felt his hackles going up, he gave me such a look! It was like a knife in the back. He probably feels that Papa would interfere in the way he ran things, and I expect he's quite right, it may well make life difficult for him for a while, but, if it makes Papa happy, Ellis will just have to grin and bear it.'

She smiled at him affectionately. 'You really care about your father, don't you?'

He went a little pink. 'He's the only one I've got!'

She laughed at his embarrassed expression, and he hurriedly went on, 'And I'm very grateful to you, Claudia. You've been such a help. I had a feeling you would be, that night Ellis took me to your family's restaurant, and he went into the kitchen and came out with soup on his hair and his jacket ... He wouldn't say what had happened, but I guessed, of course ...'

'Guessed what exactly?' She wondered what on earth he had imagined going on in the kitchen!

'Well, obviously, that he had said or done something to annoy you, and you had thrown the soup at him,' Stephen said with wide-eyed satisfaction. 'And very funny he looked, too! I didn't dare laugh, mind you. I had a feeling he might hit me. But it left me very impressed with any girl who could do that to Ellis, and I thought you might just be the girl to face up to my father, too.'

'Sometimes I wonder what sort of scientist you are!' she drily said, shaking her head.

He laughed. 'Oh, I'm good, believe me. Put me in a laboratory and I can cope with anything. It's life that is difficult.'

'Isn't that the truth?' Claudia said, grimacing.

'Anyway,' Stephen said, 'that's what made me think that if you could deal with Ellis you could deal with Papa.' He grinned at her. 'And I was right, wasn't I?'

'I'm not sure I can deal with either of them!'

'You can wrap them round your little finger!' Stephen said with cheerful amusement. 'I admire the way you deal with Ellis. He had made a big pass at you, hadn't he? He usually gets his own way with women. I like to think he doesn't get anywhere with you. It makes him more human, more like me!' He laughed at himself, grimacing, then opened the door. 'Well, I had better go and help Papa into the car. I'll see you when I drive him back. You don't mind not being invited, do you? I'd love to have you join us, but I think we should keep this discussion in the family. It could get very tense, not to say nasty, if Ellis objects.'

'I understand,' she said, only too glad not to be going, and Stephen looked down at her, his face alight.

'That's the wonderful thing about you—you always do.'

Over his shoulder she saw his father coming along slowly, with Ellis close beside him.

Claudia met the cold grey eyes which were watching her and Stephen, and a little shiver ran down her back. Ellis did not even like to see them together, just talking in a friendly way. There was threat in his face.

What right did he have to look at her like that? He was planning to take Estelle to Germany with him, he had lied to her—so why should he feel entitled to look at her with icy contempt merely because she and his brother were good friends?

On sudden, angry impulse Claudia stood on tiptoe, meaning to kiss Stephen on the cheek, but he turned his head instantly, sensing her movement and her intention, and met her mouth with his own.

It was a brief kiss, warm and sensitive, rather than earth-shattering, and a moment later Stephen turned away.

Claudia stood quite still, flushed and startled. Why had Stephen kissed her on the lips, instead of the cheek? He wasn't really attracted to her, was he? That was a complication she could not cope with! Stephen was her friend; that was how she thought of him and she would never think of him as anything else, so she hoped he had not begun to like her too much?

Her eyes flashed to Ellis and she flinched at the look in his face. He frightened her. She hadn't meant to make him jealous, only to show him that she didn't care what he did. He could go to Germany with anyone he chose, he wasn't the only man in the world!

Her pride had pushed her into kissing Stephen, but now she felt sick and miserable and she wanted to cry. Her own motives were such a tangle that she no longer knew why she did anything, but other people's motives were even less explicable. She was beginning to wish she lived on a desert island.

Ellis opened the front door, Quentin walked through it with Stephen, and, through her lashes, Claudia watched Ellis follow them, his long strides taking him further and further away rapidly. He unlocked his car and got behind the wheel, without looking back. She heard the angry burst of fire as his engine started, then he accelerated away at tremendous speed, grinding up the gravel driveway.

Stephen drove away at more leisurely pace, giving her a friendly wave and a grin. Quentin sat beside him, staring straight ahead into his dark world, but smiling slightly, as if he, at least, was very happy.

Another moment and they had both gone, and she stood there alone, feeling icy cold; shivering as she listened to the distant whisper of the river, the sound of the wind in the bare trees.

She had never felt so depressed in her entire life.

CHAPTER NINE

STEPHEN drove his father back several hours later, and stayed at the house until the evening, so that there was no work done that day, not that that mattered to Quentin. He was far too happy. Ellis had agreed that he should soon go back at work, in Switzerland, at the corporation's head offices in Geneva, and Quentin was walking on air all day, with no interest in dictating to Claudia. He could only talk about one subject, and he did, endlessly, while Stephen watched him with amused, affectionate satisfaction.

'How long would you say it would take me to finish my book? Another three months? Four?' Quentin asked Claudia. 'That will be around June, won't it? Yes... Then I think I'll put this house on the market in June—the perfect time to sell, it will look its loveliest in June. When does your contract run out, Stephen? Not long now, is it? And then you'll be coming home, too. Have you ever been to Switzerland in June, Claudia? Oh, you are going to love it. It will take your breath away.'

Claudia knew it wasn't very likely that she would see Switzerland for years to come. When Quentin had finished his book, she would go back to London, to another temporary job, to the usual round of auditions, voice training, exercises, saving every penny she could and wondering if she would ever get work in the theatre, wondering if she was wasting her time. Did she have any real talent? Was she deluding herself when she thought she had a future in the theatre? Sometimes she despaired enough to feel like giving up. That was one reason why she had had a strong fellow feeling for Quentin. They had had something in common. Both she and Quentin had been beached and without hope. Now Quentin had been rescued; he was going back into his old life, but she wasn't, she was still waiting for something to happen, and beginning to suspect that she was just wasting her life.

Stephen saw her small, wry smile and understood it. He smiled back at her and said to his father, 'You haven't talked to Claudia yet about the job, Papa.'

Quentin turned his head, his face excited and flushed. 'Haven't I? I thought I had. Claudia...' He put out his hand and she leaned over to take it. He patted her fingers, beaming. 'Claudia, my dear, how would you like to come with me?'

'With you?' she repeated, not quite sure what he meant.

'To Switzerland,' he said, holding her hand, and she drew a startled, incredulous breath, her body jerking. Quentin felt the shock run through her and tightened his grip of her.

'Switzerland? But... Why?'

'I shall need a secretary even more there,' he pointed out quietly. 'And I need someone I can trust absolutely. My work will involve reading very confidential papers, and, as I can't see to read, I'll have to rely on my secretary. The same applies to signing cheques, checking accounts... It is essential that I have someone I know to be scrupulously honest. Someone like you, Claudia.'

She flushed, very touched. 'Thank you.'

He smiled. 'Also we work well together. When I remember the stupid girls who came before you! I don't think I could bear to go through that again, trying girl after girl, and getting nowhere. I might strangle one of them! Claudia, you will think it over, won't you? I realise it would mean being a long way from your family, but I'm sure you would like Switzerland. You would get a big increase in salary, of course. Once I was back in the corporation, your workload would be different, but it would be harder, I realise that. You would have more people to deal with; instead of working in this quiet house we would be in a busy office block, with phones ringing and people coming and going all the time. And it would be a foreign country for you—you would have to learn to speak several other languages, certainly German and Italian, they would be essential, but I'd make sure you had the best of help in learning them, and you would have a flat of your own, and a phone, so that you could ring your sister, and a car.'

He broke off as Claudia gave a faint little groan. Quentin's brows worked enquiringly.

'What do you say, Claudia?' he asked.

'Oh, I . . . I'm overwhelmed, it sounds wonderful, and I'm very grateful to be asked, but . . .' She bit her lip and Stephen watched her face, frowning.

'But what?' Quentin asked anxiously. 'Claudia, please come . . . Whatever you want, I'm sure we can agree . . .'

She gave him a rueful look, then an apologetic one at Stephen, pulling a face. 'I'm sorry . . . I've loved working for you, and I wish I could go to Switzerland, but I'm not really aiming at a career in business, you know. I want to be an actress, not a secretary, and I can't leave London. If I'm not able to go for auditions I won't ever get my chance...'

Quentin's body slumped in his chair, his mouth turned down, his face disappointed. He let go of her hand and sighed.

'I'm so sorry,' Claudia said, watching him unhappily. 'I hate having to say no to you, but I've worked so hard to be an actress; it's everything I want, I can't give up yet.'

Quentin nodded heavily. 'Of course, I understand...' he said, but of course he didn't. He was being polite, but she sensed that he thought she was fooling herself about a career in the theatre, and maybe she was, but she hadn't yet reached the stage where she could contemplate giving up.

'Well, there is plenty of time yet, Papa,' Stephen gently said. 'You have to finish your book first, and that will take some months, you said? Yes? Well, then, you can see how things go.' He glanced at his watch. 'I must go now, I have a lot of work to do. Claudia, will you walk to the door with me?'

On the way, she said wryly, 'I won't change my mind, you know, Stephen. I'm sorry, but——'

'I didn't expect you would,' he interrupted. 'I just wanted to lift my father's spirits. He looked so depressed, Claudia, and I hate to see him sad. He has been much more like his old self lately; always cheerful and busy. I want him to stay that way. And, after all, does it hurt to give him some hope? And who knows what the future has in store, anyway?'

'That's true enough,' she said, sighing. 'I wonder, what if I find someone else to take over my job—and I train her over the next couple of months? That might work.'

'That's not a bad idea,' he agreed. 'OK, see if you can find a suitable girl, but she'll have to be vetted before she starts working for Papa. We have to be very careful. Anyone who works for one of us has to be thoroughly investigated.'

'I wasn't,' Claudia said light-heartedly, and Stephen gave her an odd look.

'Of course you were,' he said, and she did a double-take, not really believing him.

'You can't be serious?' She laughed, then stopped laughing as she saw his face. Then she began to frown. 'What do you mean, investigated?'

'The corporation had your entire life checked out,' he said. 'From birth to the moment I hired you. It's purely routine, Claudia—not personal at all. Everyone is checked. Don't worry, I didn't even see the papers. There was no need to—our personnel department deals with all that. I was so sure you were OK that I just went ahead and hired you. After all, you had worked for my brother, so I knew you must be suitable to work for Papa, but you still had to be vetted, because you had only worked for Ellis for a short time, as a temp. They had to do a full investigation of you before you could come and work here.'

A little shiver ran down her spine at the very idea of it. 'If I'd known! What a nightmare world to live in! But what about afterwards, do you keep someone's details on file for as long as they work for your company?'

He nodded. 'Well, obviously... That is the point of it. If there were ever reason to doubt your honesty or loyalty, we might need to know all about you very fast.'

'How horrible!' she burst out, darkly flushed. 'I hate the idea of having my whole life filed away in your secret vaults! I'm sure it's illegal. You didn't have my consent to poke and pry into my privacy.' She thought about it, frowning, then asked, 'And when I stop working for your father, will this file be destroyed?'

'Eventually,' he said in an evasive way, and she wasn't going to let him get away with hiding anything.

'What does that mean? When will they destroy my file?'

'I'm not sure, maybe five years... Or ten?'

'What?'

'After all, you might use whatever knowledge you've acquired, commit a crime... We have to protect ourselves, Claudia.'

'And me? Aren't I allowed to protect myself?' she angrily asked. 'You had no right to investigate me like that—and, if I'd known, I would never have taken the job with your father in the first place.'

'I'm sorry,' Stephen began but she turned on her heel and walked away. Before she rejoined his father, she heard his car start. A moment later and he was gone, and she felt both sorry and relieved. She liked Stephen, but she saw that there was no point in seeing much of him in the future. They had no experience, no point of view, in common.

She had thought Stephen was so different from his brother, and of course he was; but although on the surface they were not similar, there was a basic bedrock to their natures that was identical. She kept forgetting that this was a very wealthy family she had got involved with—money set them apart and made them behave in an alien fashion, see life from another

angle to her own. They found it expedient to keep
files on everyone who worked for them, and they were
quite blind to how others saw it. They had not learned
to care what anyone else thought. She had learnt that
from the start where Ellis Lefèvre was concerned,
when he locked her into his hotel suite in spite of her
angry protests. Ellis had made it crystal-clear that he
made the rules in his world, and expected everyone
else to keep them, and someone like her was of no
importance whatsoever.

She kept thinking about that file on her all day;
she thought about it even when she was in bed. She
grew so angry that she would have resigned and left
Quentin's employ, had he not been blind and de-
pendent on her, but Quentin had her at a disadvantage. She was fond of him by now, and she was
sorry for him—a fatal combination. Her anger was
not proof against Quentin next morning; he was too
happy. Every time he thought of rejoining the corporation, he could hardly stop smiling, and his happiness touched her heart.

So she stayed, and worked hard, wanting to get the
book finished in record time so that Quentin could
leave for Switzerland, and she could go back to living
in London.

That first weekend, to avoid meeting Stephen, she
took an early morning train back to London to stay
with her sister. Annette immediately noticed the
change in the arrangements for her visits, and ques-
tioned her with sisterly lack of tact.

'I don't like to rely on him for a lift, and it means
I miss a whole morning of my time off,' Claudia
evaded.

'What about the other one?' asked Annette, beating egg white until it was so stiff that when the huge bowl was turned upside down nothing fell out.

'Quentin?' Claudia asked, deliberately, and her sister gave her a wry smile.

'You know who I mean.'

Claudia did, and was half inclined not to answer, but that would in itself be some sort of admission, so she flatly said, 'Ellis is in Germany.'

'I thought he was in Japan!' Annette loved to hear about his travels and to fantasise a little about him, suspected Claudia, reluctantly replying.

'He was, but he had to go to Germany because of trouble in one of their factories.'

'When does he get back?'

'I've no idea, he doesn't keep me posted as to his movements!' Claudia tartly told her.

Annette gave her a taunting smile. 'I bet you wish he did!'

'I am not remotely interested in the man!' Claudia said, mentally crossing her fingers as she lied.

Annette began to laugh, and Claudia decided to go and help her brother-in-law chop onions for a sauce he was making.

Pierre drove her back next day, since the restaurant was not open that Sunday evening, and he and Annette felt like taking a pleasant drive by the river. They dropped Claudia at around six. Stephen had returned to Cambridge by then. Quentin said that Stephen had missed seeing her and Claudia said, 'How nice of him.' She made her voice light, but Quentin had ears like a bat and picked up the faintly dry undertone, frowning.

'You and Stephen haven't quarrelled?'

'Quarrelled? Good heavens, no,' she said, but the question enlightened her to the fact that Stephen had not indicated to his father that they had disagreed over anything.

'Well, it would surprise me if you did,' Quentin said slowly, his face wry. 'People don't quarrel with Stephen much. Ellis, now... He's a horse of a different colour. He quarrels all the time. He's very dictatorial, and that is good, in some ways. It means he has authority in the company, he gets his own way, when he needs to—but it can be bad, too. He can put backs up, particularly when he's dealing with older men, who sometimes feel he is treating them with contempt.' He stopped short, grimacing. 'I must stop doing that!' he muttered to himself, and she was puzzled, watching him.

'Doing what?'

'Talking to you so freely!' he said, his mouth crooked. 'You are insidious, girl. You're far too good at listening. I keep forgetting who I'm talking to, and I say things to you that I shouldn't. If Ellis heard me, he would think I was going senile!'

She laughed. 'Nobody would think that! Your brain is as sharp as a razor.'

The conversation underlined her realisation that she came from another world to that inhabited by the Lefèvre family. Quentin had frankly said that he should not speak so freely to her, and that Ellis would not like it, if he knew. Stephen had said she could not be trusted until her whole background had been researched and filed away. She was an inferior being, apparently; only permitted into their world on a certain level, and even then not to be trusted. It made Claudia feel bleakly depressed.

Towards the end of that week, she got a phone call from her agent, who sounded mildly cheerful, which was unusual for him. His most normal mood was one of grim despair.

'Can you get the morning off tomorrow?' he asked.

'An audition?' she guessed eagerly. 'Yes, I'm sure I can. That was part of our agreement when I took this job. Where do I go? What is it? Anything really interesting?'

'I don't know what you'll think,' he said gloomily. 'A TV ad. The product is a music centre, they say. Not very exciting. Pays well, though, and it does get your face known. Do you want to go for it?'

'Why not?' she said, her face falling in disappointment. For a second she had thought it was going to be a part in a play. 'Anything is better than not working at all.'

'That's the attitude!' approved her agent, but he sounded offhand, and she wondered if he was beginning to regret having her on his books. She wasn't making any money for him. How long now before he told her he was having to stop representing her? In the beginning, she had looked like a winner, but day by day she was turning into a loser, and he had no time for losers. 'Sorry to hurry you, angel, but I have other calls to make,' he said, wanting to move on to more important people.

Other clients he was sending to this audition? she thought with wry cynicism. He wouldn't tell her, if so, and she didn't bother to ask.

'They're apparently holding the audition at the company itself,' he explained. 'It's in Long Acre, easy to get to, a short walk from Leicester Square station, OK? You must be there at eleven. Ask in the reception lobby for a Mr Rimbaud.' He gave her the full address, said, 'Good luck, darling, let me know how you get on!' and rang off.

Claudia sat staring at the piece of paper on which she had written the address. Well, it was work, anyway. She was too desperate to care what sort of work it was, so long as it involved some sort of acting.

Quentin was perfectly happy to let her have the day off, and she got up early next day and was in London long before the specified hour of the audition, so that she could spend an hour in her sister's flat, making herself look as spectacular as possible. Annette helped, both practically and with advice, giving her a pair of sheer silk nylons, producing a favourite bottle of French perfume, doing her hair, and, when they had both done their best, boosting her ego by telling her she looked terrific.

Claudia had no idea what sort of image the advertising company would be looking for, so she had chosen her most stylish dress: a classical black wool one with a high neck, long sleeves, a narrow belt at the waist and a smooth, straight skirt which accentuated her slender figure.

'Very classy,' Annette congratulated her. 'Turn round . . . Yes, you look terrific!'

Claudia smiled gratefully. 'I shall have masses of competition, remember!'

'You'll get the job,' Annette insisted.

Claudia took another look in the mirror before she left. Well, she had done her best. Her red-gold hair was swept up at the back and pinned there with a black lace bow, her pale green eyelids shimmered faintly, her skin was cool and clear, and her full mouth was a glossy red. She knew she looked good, and that gave her the confidence to go to the audition in the right mood. After all these months of rejections and failures, she needed some sort of small success, or she would seriously think of giving up. She had been trying to get work for so long, and it was always the same—too many actors chasing too few parts. You had to be special to get anywhere, and she was beginning to wonder if she had the magic ingredients required.

'Well,' she said, smiling bravely, 'I'm as ready as I'll ever be!'

'Take a taxi,' Pierre advised. 'It will make you feel successful from the start.'

She kissed both him and her sister. 'Thanks, you two. I don't know what I'd do without you. Keep your fingers crossed for me!'

The taxi dropped her outside a high building in Long Acre, and she walked slowly through the swing doors into a spacious, carpeted reception area, where a girl sat behind a desk answering a phone while she thoughtfully studied her pink nail polish.

She glanced up at Claudia, who said, 'Mr Rimbaud?'

The receptionist picked up a clipboard, said flatly, 'Your name?' and when Claudia told her made a tick on the top sheet on the clipboard. She waved a pink-tipped finger towards the lift. 'Top floor. Door at the end of the corridor. Knock before you go in...'

Claudia would have asked her a few questions about the audition, but the other girl was talking into the phone almost without a pause. 'Oh, I know... Yes... I know...' she intoned, her eyes back on her nails, and Claudia walked away towards the lifts.

The top floor of the building was very quiet, the floors deeply carpeted. Claudia walked to the end of the corridor, as instructed, listening with faint disquiet to the silence all around her. There were several doors along the corridor, but she heard nothing from behind them. Perhaps the offices were soundproofed? Could they all be empty?

She paused outside the last door, hesitating before she knocked on it. She was strung up about the audition, full of nervous tension. That must be why she had this odd prickling sensation on the back of her neck.

She took a deep breath and knocked firmly. The door swung open a moment later, and she walked into the room, ready to smile at whoever was running the auditions, then stopped dead, not seeing anyone at all. Her eyes flashed around a luxuriously furnished sitting-room. She had been expecting an office, not that, and her nerves jumped, taking in the deep, wide white couch, strewn with jewel-coloured cushions, which was the centre of the room. She didn't like the look of that. It was far too much like a bed.

She swung on her heels, meaning to leave again, but as she did so the door was slammed shut and she froze, staring in shock at the man in an elegantly tailored pin-striped city suit, who was leaning on the door, staring back at her with a mocking smile on his hard features.

'"'Won't you walk into my parlour?' said the spider to the fly"',' murmured Ellis Lefèvre with soft amusement, but Claudia did not laugh.

She was first pale, then flushed, as it dawned on her that he had lured her here, through her agent, with talk of a phoney advertisement. It had never even occurred to her that it might not be a genuine audition. She had heard of this sort of thing happening, but her agent was usually so careful, so trustworthy. Had he been fooled too? Or had he been in on this little plot?

'Get out of my way—I am leaving!' she muttered angrily, and Ellis smiled again, slowly shaking his head.

Claudia was beginning to be frightened, remembering the silence along this corridor—was there anybody else up here on this top floor? Or were they quite alone? When she looked around the room just now she had noticed a door on the other side—where did that lead? To a bedroom?

A wave of burning colour swept up her face, she tried to think clearly, to work out what to do, while Ellis watched her with glinting, narrowed eyes.

'You look as if you need to sit down, before you fall down,' he drawled, and moved away from the door towards the couch. 'Can I get you a drink? I should have one, you're going to need it. I suggest a small brandy—that's always good for shock.'

Claudia wasn't actually listening to him; she had her eyes fixed on the door, and, as soon as he was some distance away, she feverishly shot to the door and tried to pull it open. It didn't budge. She tried again, hearing the useless grinding of the handle. She might have known he wouldn't have walked away if it hadn't been locked. She turned to stare after him as he walked to a mahogany wall cupboard and opened it, got out two fine crystal glasses, and set them out.

'You can't keep me here!' she said, and felt a dizzying sense of *déjà vu*. They had been here before;

this was a rerun of their first meeting. Was that what had put the idea into his head? Confused and flustered, she shakily said, 'What do you want?' which was about the most stupid question she could have asked, and Ellis laughed silently, pointing that out, his eyes moving down over her with sensual, disturbing intimacy.

'You,' he said.

CHAPTER TEN

'Am I supposed to be flattered?' Claudia bitterly asked, tears stinging her eyes. She knew she had given Ellis the chance to say that to her, and she was furious with herself, but she was angrier with him because he had said it. 'Well, I'm not!' she snapped, as he opened his mouth to answer her. 'In fact, I'm insulted. How many other women have heard you talk like that? It isn't flattering, knowing I'm just the latest in a long line of women you've chased. Have any of them meant a thing to you?'

He looked as if he wanted to interrupt, but she kept talking over him, her face very flushed and angry.

'No, of course they haven't. You think all women are just objects, toys for you to play with when you're in the mood. You think you can just walk in and grab what you want, and nobody will dare say no, because you're so rich and important. Well, you don't scare me, or impress me. I'm saying no, and I mean it.' He stopped smiling and began to frown, and she should have stopped there, while she was winning, but a stab of sudden jealousy made her bite out, 'So you can go back to Estelle Harding!'

His grey eyes brightened dangerously. 'Can I? Well, thank you,' he said, in the silky voice she most distrusted, and she bit down on her inner lip. She had done it again—betrayed herself. Oh, she could scream. She just wasn't in his league at this game. She kept betraying herself, letting him get glimpses of her real feelings, when she should be as cool and controlled as he managed to be.

She drew a sharp breath, lifting her chin and out-facing him, fighting to get back her icy calm. 'That's right, Mr Lefèvre, you can go back to your girlfriend. You can go anywhere, as long as you leave me alone. Obviously, you've gone to a lot of trouble to set up this situation, and I'm sorry to disappoint you, but you've wasted your time, because you aren't going to sweet-talk me into bed, so just unlock that door and let me go home, please.'

For a second, she thought Ellis was going to obey her. He stared fixedly at her, his brows level, his mouth tight, and the room reverberated with the tension in them both.

'All right,' he slowly said, then turned away and poured a finger of brandy into both glasses, carried them over to a low mahogany coffee table which stood just in front of the white couch, put down the drinks and sank backwards on to the couch, until he lay full length, his head on one arm, his feet on the one at the far end, his arms behind his head and his long body elegantly draped against the cushions.

'What are you doing?' Claudia gasped angrily, trying not to watch him, but, like a rabbit trapped by the hypnotic beam of headlights, unable to help it. Her green eyes darkened with a mixture of pain and desire. The man was the sexiest thing she had ever seen and she wanted him, which was bad enough. What was worse was that he knew exactly how she felt! His mocking smile told her so; held promise and teasing and a maddening satisfaction.

'First, we have our drink and talk,' he said.

'We've got nothing to talk about!' She turned back towards the door.

'Not even my father?' he queried, and she hesitated, frowning.

'What about him?' She searched his face with suspicious eyes. What could he possibly want to say to her about his father? 'You haven't changed your mind about his rejoining the corporation, have you?'

'I might have to,' he said coolly, and she came towards him, her face scornful.

'What do you mean, might have to? What possible reason can you have to turn him down?'

Ellis shrugged. 'Well, as you won't go to Switzerland to work for him and we can't find another secretary who is anywhere near as good as you, I really can't see how he can cope with the work he wants to do. He can't do it without a secretary, you know that. Another pair of eyes is essential, but it has to be someone he trusts and likes, and that's the problem.'

'Yes, I see that,' she said soberly. 'And I'm very sorry, but I really couldn't give up my chance of a career in the theatre. I'm sure I will be able to train someone to do what I do, though, in time.'

'No amount of training will make my father like her, whoever she may be! He was difficult enough with his secretaries, before he went blind, but these days he is impossible, and you know it. But never mind, now that he has begun to write he'll soon forget the corporation.'

'Oh, but he has his heart set on going back to work,' Claudia said unhappily. 'He is only writing this book because he's bored and restless——'

'Is it any good, do you think?' he interrupted, swinging his feet down, sitting up and leaning forward to pick up one of the glasses.

'It's wonderful,' she said with real enthusiasm. 'I'm having a wonderful time working on it with him. I'm sure it is going to be a bestseller when it comes out.'

'Really?' he said with apparent disbelief, handing her the glass.

'Yes, really!' Claudia said impatiently.

'Is your drink OK?' he asked, getting up.

'Yes, thank you,' she said looking at her brandy in a vague way, rather surprised to find herself holding it.

Ellis was standing far too close, and she was far too aware of his tall, powerful body; she hurriedly moved sideways, away from him. His mouth twisted sardonically, he drank some of the amber liquid in his glass, and then walked back to the drinks cabinet to get a refill.

'Tell me more about my father's book,' he said, over his shoulder. 'It isn't full of family skeletons? It isn't going to embarrass us all, I hope, is it?'

'Certainly not, I should think you would be proud of him, because it is such a readable, fascinating book.' Claudia sat down, talking eagerly, rather relieved that the conversation had turned this way and she could stop being afraid that at any moment Ellis would pounce. 'I told you last time you came to your father's house——' She broke off, remembering that occasion, the brief flare of happiness, of sympathy between them, until Estelle arrived on the scene and ruined everything. He had been lying to her, cheating her; he had meant to take Estelle to Germany all along even while he was asking her to meet him when he got back. She must not forget again that this was not a man you could trust.

'Told me what?' he asked, turning, his glass in his hand, to eye her quizzically.

'What a terrific writer your father is!' she bit out, despising herself because yet again she had begun to forget what he was like.

Ellis only had to smile at her, look into her eyes, for her head to swim and her brains to addle. She was such a fool over him.

'I think you did, yes, although I don't think I was listening properly; there were other things on my mind.' He paused, watching her with that intimate, mocking smile. 'You, for instance.'

She looked away, her stupid heart turning over and over, and muttered, 'Don't start that again!' then drank some of the brandy to give herself something to do with her trembling hands, but taking her eyes off him was another mistake because a second later he was sinking down beside her on the couch, sitting far too close, his long, lean body turned towards her and his thigh touching hers.

Giving a gasp of shock, Claudia almost dropped her glass, and Ellis deftly took it from her and put it down on the coffee table. He put his own down beside it, and she should have leapt up then and got away, but just as she was thinking of doing that Ellis turned and caught hold of her shoulders.

Her mouth went dry. She looked once into his eyes, then looked down, her lashes fluttering against her hot cheek. 'Don't touch me, I don't want you to touch me,' she hoarsely whispered.

'You do,' he said with utter confidence. 'You want me as much as I want you. We both knew how it was between us the first day we met. It was like a crackle of electricity, wasn't it? From the very start.' His hands softly moved down her back, stroking her, gently pushing her towards him. 'Some things are inevitable, Claudia. We were meant for each other.'

She put both hands on his chest, holding him off, her head averted. 'You may jump into bed with people all the time, but I don't!' she muttered, and he laughed softly.

'Good. I'm delighted to hear it. So long as you jump into bed with me.'

She was really scared now, shaking violently, because the ache of need inside her was getting worse every minute and she was afraid she was going to give in to him, even though she knew she would never forgive herself if she did.

'You think your money buys you anything, don't you?' she almost shouted at him. 'Well, it won't buy me. Why don't you leave me alone? Can't you see——?'

'I can see you, and only you,' he said in a thickened voice. 'Nothing else in this world, Claudia.'

And then he put a hand to her cheek, so gently that it was like the brush of a leaf, yet she flinched from it as if that light touch burned her skin and hurt more than the worst torture.

'Don't,' she pleaded. 'Please, please, don't.' But she said the last words against his fingertips as he laid them on her trembling mouth, and she was looking into his eyes and drowning in them.

'I want you so much,' he said, and she didn't doubt for an instant that he meant it.

She was fully hypnotised now, under his spell, her green eyes huge and glowing, with the black, dilated pupils in their centres shining like polished jet and reflecting his face. Ellis was pale, almost haggard, with desire, his eyes very dark, his breathing quick and rough. He looked at her mouth and his lips parted.

'Claudia,' he breathed, bending towards her, and she was drawn to him as if by a magnet, irresistibly. Their mouths met and she gave a wild moan and closed her eyes, putting her hands up to clasp his head, her fingers meeting in his thick black hair, her body bending, swaying, towards his.

Ellis put both his arms around her and held her tightly, possessively, their mouths merging, their bodies merging. They fell back on to the couch and lay there, entwined, kissing, but it wasn't enough. Claudia felt her temperature rising. She was burning for him; her hands moved restlessly, touching him, pushing back his collar, opening his shirt and sliding inside to feel the warm flesh hidden there, exploring his body without inhibition because she almost felt she was dreaming this, it wasn't really happening, it wasn't her doing these things, it was not real, it was only one of those dreams she had been having night after night for weeks. She was overwhelmed by a sensuality she had never known; she was hot and languid and unable to think about anything but this aching pleasure.

'I love you,' she groaned, her face buried in his body, and Ellis suddenly took hold of her arms and pushed her down on to her back. Startled, she opened her green eyes. He lay beside her, propped on his elbow, gazing down at her flushed, aroused face. She couldn't meet his stare, her mind filled with images of herself a few moments ago, going crazy in his arms. She had been so sure she was strong enough to keep him at arm's length, but the minute he touched her she had crumbled like sand, and she was afraid to look at him now, afraid of what she would see—the mockery and satisfaction he must be feeling. He had won. She was his, whenever he wanted to take her, and he knew it.

'Say it again,' he whispered, and she closed her eyes again, tightly, to hide the tears threatening to fall, and shook her head. How much more did he want? Hadn't he humiliated her enough?

'Claudia,' he said huskily, his fingers tracing the hot curve of her cheek. 'Darling, look at me...'

He sounded different—she was puzzled, bewildered, afraid to look and yet needing to, so she slowly opened her eyes and he looked deep into them with an expression on his face that made her heart knock wildly against her ribs.

'I'm in love with you,' he said, and Claudia thought for a second she had imagined him saying it, because it couldn't be true, could it? Ellis Lefèvre could not be in love with her. But she kept looking into his grey eyes and wondering how she could ever have thought that they were cold, and Ellis was smiling crookedly at her, passion in his face, desire, need, but more than that, a warmth and love she had to believe in, and so Claudia burst into tears.

'Claudia! Whatever is it?' Ellis asked, horrified, and she sobbed aloud.

'I always cry when I'm happy.'

He gave a choked crack of laughter, and asked, 'What do you do when you're sad? Laugh?'

'Quite often,' she said, tears running down her face, and Ellis leaned down to taste a tear with his tongue tip, sending a shiver of sensuality down her spine and making her shake from head to foot.

He kissed her cheeks, her wet eyelids, her mouth again, and she kissed him back, her tears forgotten, her passion rising again. Ellis broke off suddenly, breathing roughly, and held her down, shaking his head, smiling.

'No, we're going too fast, and I don't want to make love to you here and now, this isn't the place.'

She was struck dumb, staring back at him, and he laughed abruptly at her expression.

'Yes, I know—you thought that that was what I got you up here for?'

'Lured me, you mean!' she accused, and he nodded.

'That's right, I did. It was a well-laid plan, and it worked. I had to get you alone, where we wouldn't be interrupted and you couldn't run away. I had to make you see how it really is with us.'

'Was Joe in on it? Or did you lie to him, too?' she asked and he looked blank.

'Joe?'

'My agent.'

'Oh, him. No, one of our companies is an advertising agency. They own this building, in fact. This floor is usually in use as a studio, but I've commandeered the whole floor for today. The company keep this little flat in case visiting foreign executives need a place in London to stay, or for private entertaining...'

Jealousy caught her on the raw, but she fought to hide it, lifting her brows in a pretence of cynicism. 'Oh, yes? And how often have you used it for private entertaining?'

'I don't need to,' he said, his gaze understanding and wry. 'Claudia, I have my own flat here, remember?'

'Yes,' she said, pain eating at her. 'That's where you take your women, usually, of course. How long does it usually last with you? Days? Weeks? Months?' She bit down on her lip to stop herself crying again, then burst out, 'It won't work out. You know it wouldn't last, and I don't want to get hurt, that isn't the sort of love-affair I want for myself, Ellis. I'm not the sophisticated type, I can't just go into an affair and shrug and walk away afterwards, as your other women do. I want a lover who will stay with me.'

'Don't we all?' he said, stroking her hair. 'What do you think I want? Someone who will leave me next week? Darling, you haven't listened . . . I love you.'

She was afraid to believe him, even though it made her so happy she felt she could walk on the ceiling, float like a balloon.

She frowned at nothing, and asked him, 'What lies did you tell poor Joe?'

'Joe?' he asked again, just as blank, and she scolded him.

'Now who doesn't listen? My agent—what fairy-stories did you spin for him?'

'I didn't. The advertising agency got in touch and said they were interested in hiring you for a TV commercial, told him to send you along this morning for an interview.'

She felt her cheeks burning again. 'God knows what they thought you were up to!'

He grinned shamelessly. 'Oh, I know, too. They thought——'

'All right, it's obvious,' she crossly told him. 'My reputation will be zero by tomorrow. Everyone will think I'm your latest woman.'

'Aren't you?' he mocked and she bit her lip.

'Not yet,' she said. 'I still have time to get away.'

'No, you don't,' he assured her. 'You're mine now, and for as long as we love each other, and don't ask me how long that will be, because time is as long as it lasts, you can't measure it or prophesy when it will end.'

He got up suddenly, raking back his black hair, buttoning his shirt again. 'Now, tidy yourself and do something about your make-up, then we'll go and have some lunch and talk.'

Claudia scrambled up, taken aback by this sudden change of mood. She wasn't sure exactly what Ellis was up to, but she found her bag and ran a brush over her hair, renewed her make-up, straightened her clothes.

'We have plans to make,' Ellis said, watching her, and she shot him a secret look in her compact mirror, her heart beating faster as she saw him. How long had she loved him like this? She was only just admitting it, but when had it begun? From the first instant she saw him?

'What plans?' she asked casually, smoothing glossy lipstick on to her mouth.

'For the future,' he said, unlocking the door and standing back to let her walk past. 'Ours.' He drew her hand through his arm in a possessive gesture, and Claudia was too happy to ask any more questions. She was moving in a dream and she didn't want to wake up.

Ellis had a car parked at the back of the building; a streamlined, sleek blue sports car into which she slid with a little sigh of pleasure in the cool, eggshell-blue leather upholstery, deep and luxurious. Ellis started the ignition, there was an immediate surge of power, and they moved away. Claudia watched his long, slim hands on the wheel, her throat beating with an excited pulse as she remembered how those hands had felt when they touched her. He was very close to her, in the interior of the car, his shoulder brushing hers, his thigh inches away from her own, and her whole body vibrated with awareness of him.

It didn't even occur to her to ask him where they were going, and when he slowed down and began to back into a parking place she looked out of the window abstractedly. It was only then that she realised where they were, and her eyes opened wide.

'Are we eating here?'

'Why not? The chef is good.' He slid her a wicked look, grinning. 'I can specially recommend the cold cucumber soup.'

She laughed. 'I'm sorry, but you deserved that.'

'You're a violent woman,' he said with apparent satisfaction, then he got out of the car and so did Claudia.

'But have you booked? They may not have a table free,' she said, as they walked towards the restaurant.

'I booked,' he said, opening the door only to find his way barred by Annette and Pierre in his white chef's hat. Ellis repeated with a smile, 'I have a booking, for a table for two——'

'I'm sorry, but there has been some mistake—we are already fully booked,' Annette said with icy hostility. Pierre didn't say anything but he loomed behind her in a threatening manner, his arms folded, ready to repel Ellis if he tried to force an entry.

Realising that neither of them had noticed her yet, Claudia moved up behind Ellis's shoulder, and saw her sister's jaw drop. 'Claudia?' Annette gasped.

Pierre took off his white hat and fanned himself with it, making Gallic noises of fury and reproach.

'Can we come in?' Claudia asked Annette, who was looking from her to Ellis in wild surmise.

'What's going on?' Annette wanted to know first, not moving out of the way.

'We want to eat lunch,' Ellis answered for Claudia, his mouth crooked with amusement.

Annette ignored him. 'Why are you with him?' she asked her sister. 'I thought you hated the sight of him.'

'You know what they say,' Ellis drawled. 'Hate and love are two sides of the same coin.'

Annette's eyes rounded and her mouth opened in a gasp. 'Claudia?' she asked, staring at her sister fixedly. 'Are you...? You aren't, are you?'

'Aren't what?' Claudia said, very pink and not able to meet Annette's eyes.

'Do we have to have this conversation on the doorstep? Can't we come in?' Ellis asked, taking a step forward, and Annette fell back, letting them into the restaurant.

'If anyone is interested,' said Pierre with awful dignity, putting his white hat back on his head, 'I am going back to my kitchen.' With that he stalked away, but nobody watched him go, because his wife only had eyes for her sister, and Claudia was laughing shyly, pulling a face because she didn't know what to say to Annette.

There were a few other customers sprinkled around the tables, all of them staring too, and Claudia was very aware of that audience. She muttered to Annette, 'Look, we'll talk later, OK?'

'But are you and he...?' Annette whispered with single-minded insistence, and Claudia sighed and at last gave a nod.

'I suppose so.'

Ellis put an arm around her waist, drew her close, gave Annette a mocking little smile. 'I'm going to take your sister away to Switzerland,' he said firmly. 'Now—which is our table?'

'In that corner, for two,' Annette said absently, then repeated, 'Switzerland? You're going to Switzerland?'

'Take me to Switzerland?' Claudia thought aloud, looking at him sharply. 'Was that what you meant by having to make plans? About our future?'

'Shall we sit down and have lunch before we discuss all that?' Ellis suggested, steering her towards the table in the corner, past a couple so interested in their conversation that the woman had a forkful of spaghetti in one hand and her mouth open ready to receive it, without the food ever arriving, while she stared at them. Ellis paused to smile down at her coldly. 'I should eat your lunch before it gets cold,' he said. 'You can always catch the next show.'

The woman went red, her hand wavered and dropped her spaghetti, which spilled into her lap. She gave a shriek of horror. 'Oh, this dress will be ruined!' She leapt up, almost knocking Claudia over, and brushed the clinging strands from her silk skirt, while her companion got to his feet, scowling at Ellis.

'Now look what you've done! That dress is real silk—it cost me a fortune.'

'I didn't lay a hand on the lady,' Ellis said coolly. 'I wouldn't dream of it.'

The woman gave an offended squeak, and her companion snarled. 'Do you want a punch on the nose?'

By now, nobody was eating—everyone was watching with open fascination and enjoyment, and, realising that another big scene had developed, Annette intervened hurriedly, grabbing Claudia by the arm and tugging at her.

'Go into the kitchen, I'll deal with this.'

Ellis was still confronting the other man, ready for a fight if one broke out. Annette gave him an impatient look. 'And take him with you,' she told her sister, who took hold of Ellis and pulled him, reluctantly, out of the restaurant into the kitchen. Pierre gave them a sideways look, then went on with the veal he was cooking, turning his back deliberately.

'Every time you come here, there's a big scene,' Claudia said and Ellis bent to kiss her quickly on the mouth.

'I'm sorry, I didn't start a scene deliberately, I just got angry when I saw that woman staring at us, bolt-eyed.'

'I know,' she said, ruefully, looking at the hard angles of his face and realising that he was always going to be aggressive and hard to manage; that was his nature. Then she remembered what they had been talking about before the little scene happened, and she asked him, 'You didn't make love to me just to get me to take that job with your father in Switzerland, did you?' It wasn't a serious question—every instinct she had told her that Ellis hadn't been acting when they made love. It had been too real to be phoney, the feeling in him—but he was capable of using his own emotions to win an argument, all the same, and she still didn't trust him.

'What a devious mind you have,' Ellis said, watching her in his turn. 'No, Claudia. If you really don't want to take the job with my father, then don't, but I want you in Switzerland, because I spend more time there than anywhere else, and I want you with me as much as possible. You know how much I travel. I don't like doing it, but it is necessary, and I'm going to miss you badly when I'm away, I can't keep coming to London, we would hardly ever see each other if you lived here. You must come with me back to my home, in Switzerland.' He paused, grinned. 'Of course, you might be bored when I wasn't there, so it might be a good idea for you to work for my father.'

'Oh, yes?' she said, her face wry. 'You call me de-vious? What do you call yourself?'

'In love,' he said, cupping her face in his hands and kissing her nose.

'Not in my kitchen!' growled Pierre from the other side of the room.

Annette appeared, gave them a scolding look. 'Well, I got rid of the other couple, but it cost us the price of their meal so far, and they won't come back here, so we've lost their custom for good. You really are a nuisance, Mr Lefèvre. Every time you come here there seems to be a scene.'

'Put the price of the other couple's meal on my bill,' Ellis said. 'I'm sorry, Annette, and call me Ellis, please. We are going to know each other very well in the future, you might as well get used to that.'

'Oh,' Annette said breathlessly, signalling wild en-quiry to Claudia with her eyebrows.

Ellis looked amused. 'Shall we go and eat?' he asked Claudia, who was blushing, and looking harassed, and she nodded gratefully, glad to escape from her sister's rampant curiosity.

They took a long time choosing their meal and ate it at leisure, absorbed in their own company and unaware by then of everyone else in the room. There was so much to ask, so much to tell each other. Claudia wanted to know everything about him, and he seemed to feel the same way; he asked question after question, listening with intent interest to her answers.

One thing she had to know about was his relationship with Estelle, although she knew he would immediately suspect her of being jealous. Since she was, she admitted it almost defiantly, and Ellis gave her an amused, smiling look.

'Estelle and I had a brief fling some years ago,' he admitted. 'It wasn't me who ended it, actually, it was her. She suddenly dumped me. I wasn't expecting it and it hurt. It was a bad time for me. She met a Texan billionaire and went off to the States with him, but that didn't work out, and she came back and rang me up again.' He pulled a wry face. 'By then, though, I'd got over her and was busily engaged elsewhere and I wasn't interested. Oh, we stayed friends, I've known her for years, her and her whole family. We move in the same circles, have the same friends, we meet all the time. But as far as I was concerned our affair was over.'

'I didn't get the impression Estelle felt the same,' she said. 'And you just took her to Germany! If your affair was over, why did you do that?'

'I didn't,' he said. 'Her father did. He was going, too—didn't you realise that? There were half a dozen of us—five men, and Estelle, and she was only along for the ride. I barely set eyes on her while I was there, I was much too busy working.'

'She made it sound as if . . .' Claudia began, re-lieved and yet still not entirely certain of him.

'I know,' he grimaced. 'That's her technique. Estelle never gives up hope of wearing me down. After all, I haven't married, which makes her think I might still be carrying a torch for her. She's not the only one. If you are a single male, that makes you the target for every husband-hunting female around. Estelle knows I was interested in her once, and she hoped she could get me again if she hung around long enough. She's persistent and tenacious, and I can't avoid seeing a lot of her since her father has a lot of business contact with me, but I am not in love with her, nor have I been her lover for years, Claudia.'

She believed him then, slackening in relief, and he put a hand across the table to seize hers. 'There is no other woman in my life, I promise you, there hasn't been for some time. There is only you.'

They sat in silence for a moment, looking into each other's eyes, and then Annette's shadow fell across the table and they both started, looking round.

'More coffee? Or have you finished? But don't let me hurry you,' she said, and that was when they re-alised that everyone else had gone and they were the last customers in the restaurant.

Claudia gave a gasp. 'I promised your father I'd be back in time to get some work done before dinner!' she said, looking at her watch and seeing that it was nearly four o'clock.

'I'll drive you back,' Ellis told her, and to Annette said, 'Can I have my bill?'

'It's on the family,' Annette expansively assured him, all smiles.

Claudia could see what was in her mind. Annette heard wedding bells. How was she going to break it to her that a wedding was not being discussed?

'Why, thank you,' Ellis said gravely. 'Perhaps you and Pierre will let me return the hospitality very soon? We'll be in touch.'

Annette focused her insistent gaze on her sister. 'Give me a ring soon,' she said with a hidden touch of menace, and Claudia inwardly groaned at the questions she could see in her sister's excited eyes.

Ellis got up and held out a hand to Claudia. 'Shall we go, then? We have a lot to tell my father.'

'You have a lot to tell me,' Annette pointedly said, following them to the door, but Ellis just laughed and a moment later they were out of the restaurant and climbing into the blue sports car. Pierre had joined Annette at the door; both of them gazed enviously at the car as it shot away. Claudia waved, feeling her sister's furious vibrations at her back. Annette was dying to get her on her own, to ask endless questions, but Claudia wasn't going to know what to say to her. Come to that, what was Quentin going to make of their new relationship—would he be shocked, angry, disapproving? She knew how old-fashioned he was about some things; he had often made disapproving comments about his son's way of life.

She sat in silence most of the way out of central London, worried about what might be said when they got back, and Ellis seemed wrapped in thoughts, too, much happier than her own, it appeared, since he was whistling as he drove, and smiling to himself. He apparently did not dread his father's reaction, but then he must have had so many affairs in the past which Quentin knew about.

She had never had an affair before. She had had boyfriends, but she had never deliberately begun a love-affair which she knew could never end in marriage. Of course, she hadn't ever felt she wanted to marry anyone before, that hadn't really entered into any relationship she had had—but she wouldn't have ever imagined herself getting involved with someone like Ellis. She wasn't the sophisticated type—she didn't know how she would cope with being his lover. He was always in the public eye, everyone would know, and there would be so much talk, a spotlight on them . . . Could she bear it?

When they arrived, Ellis parked his car, took her hand and led her like a lamb to the slaughter into the house. Celeste met them in the corridor, immediately stared at those linked hands, her eyebrows going up.

"E is waiting for you, in 'is study," she said, her accent thickening as usual when she was surprised.

Claudia was flushed and uneasy; she couldn't meet Celeste's curious stare, and was half tempted to run away, to her own room, to hide, but Ellis didn't slacken his grip of her, he strode away towards his father's room, pulling Claudia reluctantly after him. He flung open the door and they both stood there looking towards the desk behind which Quentin sat, a Braille book open in front of him, his fingers busy on the raised dots.

He looked up at once, his blind face intent. 'Yes? Who is it?'

Ellis answered. 'Ellis, Papa.' He paused, lifting Claudia's hand briefly to his mouth to kiss it, smiling at her, then said, 'I've brought you my future wife, Papa.'

It was hard to tell who was most surprised. Claudia was too shaken to say a word; she just stared up at Ellis, trembling. Quentin stood up, his gnarled hands gripping the edge of his desk, looking as shaken and incredulous as Claudia did.

'Your future wife...' he repeated huskily, 'Ellis, I couldn't be more pleased... But who...?'

'Claudia,' Ellis said quietly, and she watched the old man anxiously, not knowing how he would react. He must have been expecting his eldest son to make some grand, magnificent marriage. He might be appalled at the prospect of welcoming his own temporary secretary as his daughter-in-law.

Quentin sat down abruptly, his face blank. There was a long silence and Claudia wanted to cry. He was furious, he was horrified. He was not going to welcome her.

Then Quentin got to his feet again and shakily made his way around the desk. He stopped a few feet away from them, and held out both hands, a smile curving his mouth.

'Claudia...' he said huskily. 'My dear, dear girl...'

HARLEQUIN *Romance*®

**HARLEQUIN ROMANCE
LOVES BABIES!**

And next month's title in

THE BRIDAL COLLECTION

brings you *two* babies—and, of course, a wedding.

**BOTH OF THEM
by Rebecca Winters**

THE BRIDE objected.
THE GROOM insisted.
THE WEDDING was for the children's sake!

Available this month in
THE BRIDAL COLLECTION

**LOVE YOUR ENEMY
by Ellen James**

Harlequin Romance #3202
Available wherever
Harlequin Books are sold.

WED-3

Harlequin Presents®

Coming Next Month

#1471 WHEN THE DEVIL DRIVES Sara Craven
Joanna knows there'll be a day of reckoning between herself and Cal Blackstone. And it means she'll have to make a tough decision because Cal holds all the best cards. If she refuses his demands, her family will suffer—but the price he wants her to pay is far too high.

#1472 THE SEDUCTION OF KEIRA Emma Darcy
When Keira returns to Australia, her cousin welcomes her with open arms, it seems he needs her to seduce a rival. Keira agrees to do her best, but before she has the chance, she meets Nick Sarazan, the man of her dreams. And he loses no time in seducing Keira.

#1473 NIGHTS OF DESIRE Natalie Fox
Carrie comes to Spain to look for a missing boyfriend and finds Alex Drayton instead. Soon she's working for him, then she's dreaming about him. Carrie knows it's only a matter of time before he becomes her entire world....

#1474 AN UNEQUAL PARTNERSHIP Rosemary Gibson
Mike refuses to abandon the airline business her grandfather built—especially to a cold, calculating businessman like Luke Duncan. Luke is not a man who's easily thwarted, but perhaps it's time he's taught a few of life's lessons.

#1475 RISK OF THE HEART Grace Green
Capri is determined to avoid her father's heavy-handed matchmaking attempts and have a real holiday this year. For a short while, maybe she can have some fun, instead of spending all her time fighting off rich admirers. Then she meets Taggart Smith—a man who changes everything!

#1476 SECOND TIME LOVING Penny Jordan
Daniel Forbes is attractive and charming, and he's made it clear he's attracted to Angelica. But after a bad experience with gold digger Giles, Angelica has vowed not to let another man make a fool of her. But, try as she might, she finds Daniel impossible to resist.

#1477 DARK GUARDIAN Rebecca King
Stranded on a desert island with the mysterious Brand Carradine is not as romantic as it sounds. At least that's Fliss's first reaction to her predicament. After all, Brand is her legal guardian!

#1478 NO WAY TO BEGIN Michelle Reid
Nina despises Anton Lakitos. She's convinced that the arrogant Greek property developer's interest in the family business has ruined her father's health. That's not her only problem. Anton is hell-bent on acquiring Nina, too—even if he has to use blackmail to do so.

Available in July wherever paperback books are sold, or through Harlequin Reader Service:

In the U.S.
P.O. Box 1397
Buffalo, NY
14240-1397

In Canada
P.O. Box 603
Fort Erie, Ontario
L2A 5X3

"GET AWAY FROM IT ALL" SWEEPSTAKES

HERE'S HOW THE SWEEPSTAKES WORKS

NO PURCHASE NECESSARY

To enter each drawing, complete the appropriate Official Entry Form or a 3" by 5" index card by hand-printing your name, address and phone number and the trip destination that the entry is being submitted for (i.e., Carmel Bay, Canyon Ranch or London and the English Countryside) and mailing it to: Get Away From It All Sweepstakes, P.O. Box 1397, Buffalo, New York 14269-1397.

No responsibility is assumed for lost, late or misdirected mail. Entries must be sent separately with first class postage affixed, and be received by: 4/15/92 for the Carmel Bay Vacation Drawing, 5/15/92 for the Canyon Ranch Vacation Drawing and 6/15/92 for the London and the English Countryside Vacation Drawing. Sweepstakes is open to residents of the U.S. (except Puerto Rico) and Canada, 21 years of age or older as of 5/31/92.

For complete rules send a self-addressed, stamped (WA residents need not affix return postage) envelope to: Get Away From It All Sweepstakes, P.O. Box 4892, Blair, NE 68009.

"GET AWAY FROM IT ALL" SWEEPSTAKES

HERE'S HOW THE SWEEPSTAKES WORKS

NO PURCHASE NECESSARY

To enter each drawing, complete the appropriate Official Entry Form or a 3" by 5" index card by hand-printing your name, address and phone number and the trip destination that the entry is being submitted for (i.e., Carmel Bay, Canyon Ranch or London and the English Countryside) and mailing it to: Get Away From It All Sweepstakes, P.O. Box 1397, Buffalo, New York 14269-1397.

No responsibility is assumed for lost, late or misdirected mail. Entries must be sent separately with first class postage affixed, and be received by: 4/15/92 for the Carmel Bay Vacation Drawing, 5/15/92 for the Canyon Ranch Vacation Drawing and 6/15/92 for the London and the English Countryside Vacation Drawing. Sweepstakes is open to residents of the U.S. (except Puerto Rico) and Canada, 21 years of age or older as of 5/31/92.

For complete rules send a self-addressed, stamped (WA residents need not affix return postage) envelope to: Get Away From It All Sweepstakes, P.O. Box 4892, Blair, NE 68009.

© 1992 HARLEQUIN ENTERPRISES LTD.

SWP-RLS

"GET AWAY FROM IT ALL"

Brand-new Subscribers-Only Sweepstakes

OFFICIAL ENTRY FORM

This entry must be received by: May 15, 1992
This month's winner will be notified by: May 31, 1992
Trip must be taken between: June 30, 1992—June 30, 1993

YES, I want to win the Canyon Ranch vacation for two. I understand the prize includes round-trip airfare and the two additional prizes revealed in the BONUS PRIZES insert.

Name _____

Address _____

City _____

State/Prov. _____ Zip/Postal Code _____

Daytime phone number _____
(Area Code)

Return entries with invoice in envelope provided. Each book in this shipment has two entry coupons — and the more coupons you enter, the better your chances of winning!
© 1992 HARLEQUIN ENTERPRISES LTD.   2M-CPN